Murder
at the
Matinee

B

Brabinger

Printed and bound in Great Britain by Clays Ltd. Elcograf S.p.A.

ISBN 9781739762247 (paperback)
ISBN 9781739762254 (eBook)

Published by Brabinger Publishing, London
brabinger.co.uk

To all the Gaiety boys and girls
with their tales of love, laughter and happy ever after

1934

The Gaiety Theatre

London

Chapter One

The lights blinked out on the London Underground carriage, leaving Bertie in darkness. A blinding white flash, which came from outside the window, cast an eerie illumination across the scene for a fraction of a second before the darkness returned. After a few moments the lights flickered back on. A familiar loud, low thrum beneath his feet restarted and the train lurched onwards again. Above his head the empty strap-hangers swung back and forth, reaching out to the hands of the passengers who weren't there. Bertie was the only person in the carriage.

The short branch line that ran from Holborn to Aldwych was rarely used by anyone. Perhaps they didn't bother to maintain it at the same level as the rest of the line, which might explain the flickering lights and the jolting ride. Bertie wondered whether the original intention for the line was to go somewhere further afield – rather than just the one stop it currently ran – but he was unable to give it much thought. His mind was distracted by something else: the panicked phone call he had received earlier that day.

If you believed what had been written about them in the newspapers, Alice Crawford was an enemy of his. However, this wasn't quite the truth, because their rivalry was quite friendly. As playwrights go, they were both evenly matched. One could argue that Alice was further ahead in the rankings because she'd had two more plays produced in the West End than he had. Someone else might argue that Bertie had racked up more performances in total and that meant he had done slightly better. Either way, the two of them were both playwrights at the top of their game. Still, when he picked up the phone that morning it was a rather unexpected surprise to hear her voice.

'Something's terribly wrong with the play.' She sounded flustered. 'I don't know what it means, but I think something awful is going to happen.'

It wasn't unusual for playwrights, directors or actors to get nervous as an opening night approached. In fact, the only people who were usually able to hold their nerve as the first performance loomed nearer were the stage crew, under the calm guidance of their stage manager. They'd seen it all before.

Bertie knew that if you wanted to know the real measure of your play, it was the stage crew you'd need to ask. Unlike your fellow cast members or other theatrical friends, you could always count on a backstage worker to give you the full, unvarnished truth. And when you were stuck on a tricky plot point or staging dilemma, you'd be wise to ask the head flyman or master carpenter for their opinion. They usually had one and, more often than not, it was an opinion that would be worth listening to.

The voice that he could hear down the phone line was markedly different – this wasn't opening night nerves; the opening night of Alice's play had already come and gone. In fact, the play was about to come to the end of a very successful run. No, this was something else. It sounded like genuine fear. It put Bertie on edge.

'I don't know who else I can talk to,' said Alice. 'You're the only person I know that has, well, any kind of experience with this sort of thing. Please could you stop by the theatre as soon as you can?'

Bertie had agreed and said he would do anything he could to help, but that he really needed to know what she was talking about.

Alice asked him if he'd looked at his copy of *The Era*, which had been published earlier that week. He hadn't. It was sitting folded neatly on his desk, where his efficient secretary had left it for him. Turning to the back few pages he scanned the advertisements before something caught his eye.

'Yes, I see,' he replied, gravely, down the line. Then he

uttered the words that he was already certain he would regret. 'What do you want me to do?'

The Underground carriages finally slowed and shuddered to a stop, the brakes screeching and echoing off the tiled platform walls. The doors clattered open and he made his way towards the exit. It looked like there were only two other passengers who had joined him on the short journey. This quiet station didn't require a full-length train; the three cars they had just arrived in barely took up half the platform. He looked back at the yawning black hole through which he had just travelled. An ominous void waited there, ready to swallow the metal carriages whole, for their return journey. It felt depressingly symbolic of the situation he was about to walk right into.

Bertie had been mulling everything over during the slow journey down. While he hadn't expected to arrive at the theatre with the problem solved, he had hoped that he would have been able to think of some useful insight or have some sort of explanation to offer. The truth was, the further he had travelled along the track, the more muddled his thoughts had become and the further away he seemed to find himself from any kind of answer. He still had no idea how he was going to be of any use.

The noise of the metal lattice gate being closed by the lift attendant brought him out of his thoughts; his feet had carried him automatically along the underground passages and into the trapezoidal-shaped cabin, which had been waiting, already open, for the new arrivals. As they made creaky progress up the lift shaft, he noticed a poster that had been neatly pasted on the wall. It advertised the opening night of Alice's play, twelve weeks ago. The dates on the poster indicated that the show's last two performances were today.

Bertie recalled the advert that she had drawn his attention to over the phone. It had been tucked away in the back of the newspaper.

BEWARE PATRONS OF THE MATINEE PERFORMANCE OF
ALICE CRAWFORD'S LATEST THRILLING PLAY:

TIME TO KILL

A TERRIFYING AND VERY REAL MURDER WILL BE
COMMITTED IN THE THIRD ACT.

In fact, if it hadn't been so unnoticeable, Bertie would have just assumed it was a clever ploy by the producer, but here it was hidden away, printed in simple plain text so that it blended in with its surroundings. If it had been placed as part of a promotional campaign, surely a production bearing Alice Crawford's name would have been able to place a more professional-looking advert.

Bertie walked out of the entrance to Aldwych Station. It only took a few short steps along the pavement before the Gaiety Theatre came into view, emerging from behind St Mary le Strand Church.

The bright midday sun was bearing down and he blinked a few times, his eyes still adjusting to the outdoors. It was clear to him that no one connected to the production could have placed that advert. It wouldn't have made any sense. He could still hear Alice's voice in his head, her words repeating over and over.

'But Bertie, there *is* no murder in the third act of my play.'

Chapter Two

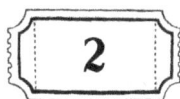

Bertie crossed over the busy Strand and skirted the edge of the theatre, walking underneath the iron awning that hung over the pavement. Strips of paper, lightly tinted pink, were printed with the bold words *final performances*. They had been pasted over the posters that lined the outside walls of the building. Perhaps counterintuitively, advertising that a show was coming to a close would usually have the effect of causing a last-minute swell in audience numbers. The subtle threat that you might miss out on the production would often convince the last few stragglers to finally go out and buy their ticket.

As he rounded the corner, approaching the curved entrance at the front of the building, he saw a woman come into view with a worried expression fixed on her face. Alice Crawford had a dominating figure, her height accentuated as she was positioned at the top of the theatre's steps. She leaned out of one of the entrance doors, grasping the edge of the frame with one hand to make sure she didn't get shut out. Almost birdlike in her appearance, her eyes darted around, searching up and down the many different roads that met in front of the theatre, unsure of the direction that Bertie would be arriving from. When she finally saw him approaching, her worried expression faded and was replaced with one of relief. He climbed the couple of steps at the front of the building, joining her on the top one.

Letting go of the door, she threw both arms around him. 'Bertie! I'm so glad you're here.'

Breaking out of the hug, Bertie rested his hands on her broad shoulders in an attempt at calming her down. Whether it was her nerves before a performance or excitement at a new idea, he had always found Alice barely able to contain the emotions that were constantly fizzing away under the surface. Much like the hair on her head, streaked with wisps of grey, which would usually be twisted up in a messy bun and secured in place with a spare pencil, it could never be fully restrained. There would always be a stray strand or two poking out.

A panicked look suddenly returned to Alice's face as she realised the door behind her was slowly closing. She spun around on the spot, managing to quickly stick a leg out and stop the door from clicking shut. 'Don't want to be locked out, do we? Not now you're finally here to save the day.'

'Well, let's not get overconfident. I'm still not sure what I can do,' said Bertie. 'But if I can do something, anything – even if that's just be here for you – then I will.'

She led him through the front doors of the building into the circular crush room. She spoke quickly, half in excitement, half in relief. 'Of course, you're just what we need. Our very own detective. You've got exactly the right sort of mind for this.'

Even with the words spilling out of her in a nervous tumble, she still talked in her trademark style with the crisp, booming confidence of a games mistress.

'Alice, I'm a writer, not a detective. Just because I got mixed up with that murder in Brighton last year, it doesn't make me an expert. It was just luck. Bad luck.'

Alice stopped and turned to face him. 'Poppycock. It was no such thing. It was bloody brilliant from what I've heard. You can't keep a secret in our business, you know. We've all heard the stories.'

'Well, yes. That's the problem with stories when they get spread around in our theatrical circles. They become more ... well, theatrical.'

She held a finger up to stop him talking further. 'Modesty is a sin,' she said, then added with a little less confidence, 'and if it isn't then it should be.' She smiled. 'You should take pride in your achievements, Bertie.'

He looked around the circular room. On the walls there were six painted panels, each occupied by a full-length portrait of a former Gaiety favourite – all of them women. It left him feeling outnumbered. Besides, there was often very little point in arguing with Alice once she had made up her mind on something.

'I do,' he said. 'I'm just saying… I want to make sure that your expectations are in check. I'll do what I can, but it might not be that much. Have you at least called the police?'

Alice paced around the room while she spoke. It left Bertie in the middle of the room, turning on the spot. 'Oh yes, the useless constable they sent round. Useless Bobby the bobby, that's what I've been calling him. He didn't seem to think much of it. Barely took an interest at all.' She stopped circling and looked at Bertie with a hopeless sort of expression. 'And this morning, an anonymous note appeared at the stage door making the same threat again.'

'No one saw who left it?'

'No, nobody's admitted to it, anyway. At least it made the police take slightly more interest in the matter; it's certainly made everyone here stand up and pay attention. Our dear Bobby said he'd go away and "make enquiries", whatever that means. I don't know what enquiries they could possibly be making, but there you go. I don't imagine that anything will come of that. Bertie, you're our only hope.'

He raised an eyebrow and opened his mouth to speak. Before he could utter a word, he was cut off by Alice, who had put up a hand in protest.

'At the very least, you'll be able to put my mind at rest, perhaps the company's minds at rest. With that useless policeman, we've got nothing to work with here. Bertie, at least you're *something*.'

'Look, Alice, I'm here for moral support and I'm happy to provide it, although I don't know that I'm about to prevent any crimes. I suppose you've already entertained the possibility that this might just be one big practical joke.'

She gave a disapproving frown at the idea. 'Yes, that's what the police's professional opinion was too. I disagree of course... Is there anyone's ear you can bend, to get them to take it more seriously?' She swallowed, then posed her question delicately. 'What about that detective friend of yours? Are you still in touch with him?'

Bertie gave a sigh. 'That's a long story that I think is best saved for another time.'

'Understood,' said Alice with a gentle nod. Despite her occasionally brash demeanour, he knew that she could be tactful when she really wanted to be.

In fact, the story he was avoiding telling wasn't that long. It was just that Bertie would rather swerve that conversation, instead of having to think about the silence that had grown between him and his friend Hugh. The sad truth was that they hadn't been in touch, let alone seen each other, since the events in Brighton nearly six months ago.

Bertie had left a couple of telephone messages with the porter at Hugh's apartment building, but his calls had not been returned. Before they had got tangled up together in solving a murder case in Brighton, they hadn't seen each other since their schooldays. Even so, they weren't exactly strangers; they had always stayed in touch by writing letters. Now any letters that Bertie sent received no response.

There was always the possibility of visiting Hugh at his flat. Even though Bertie had never been there, he had the address from their correspondence. However, he had very quickly put that idea out of his mind. If Hugh wanted to leave behind the events that had happened in Brighton, then Brighton was where they would stay.

He gave a nod towards to the door in front of them. 'Would you like to lead on?'

Alice turned to her left, ignoring the door that he had just indicated and instead led him up a set of stairs that – judging by the signs – was the way up to the dress circle. At the top of the staircase, they passed through a small foyer and entered the back of the circle on the left-hand side. The raked seating gradually fell away in front of them, a gently rolling landscape that led their gaze down towards the stage.

Bertie followed Alice down the side aisle and the shallow steps that ran down towards the front. They came to a stop a couple of rows from the end. An ominous feeling crept over him, which wasn't helped by the gloomy atmosphere that the scenery of the play seemed to evoke. The stage was a dark void of modernist set design. A seamless cyclorama had been painted in layers of textured, dark tones. It gave the impression that someone had attacked it with one huge paintbrush. The taut cloth encircled the playing space, its colours darkening as they reached the extremities, making the stage look like it went on forever.

Large flat steps dominated the design, sweeping across the floor diagonally, creating a heavy, oppressive mood that bore down on the actors that were gathered on the stage. It did nothing to alleviate the tense atmosphere that seemed to hold the room in a tight grip.

The cast appeared to be in something of a standoff. They were gathered on one side of the stage staring intently at a man who was talking to them, although it might have been fairer to say that he was pleading with them. Even though Bertie and Alice were watching on from a distance in the auditorium, the excellent acoustics of the theatre meant they could hear every word floating out towards them.

'... not a threat. As I've said, the police are convinced it's nothing more than a practical joke.'

Alice whispered some words of explanation into Bertie's ear. 'Gareth James, or is it James Gareth? I never can quite remember. Theatre manager. I'm fairly sure he wants everything to go ahead. They had a long run of bad shows before we showed up with this one. I don't think he wants to turn down the chance that he might actually make some money for once.'

Another male voice spoke up from the other side of the stage. He laughed at the absurdity of the situation. 'Well, that's easy for you to say. You're not the one who is being forced to perform, worrying that someone might drop dead at any moment. The situation is quite intolerable.'

Alice didn't have to give any words of explanation for this speaker; Bertie had already recognised him. 'Anthony Debenham? I thought he had fallen off the map in recent years?'

'Yes, well the Debenhams came as a pair – Anthony and Katherine – their agent's idea really. We thought, why not? She's doing very well for herself and of course Anthony was always a very good actor. It's nice to have a husband-and-wife team involved; it looks good on the poster, don't you think?'

The theatre manager was trying to keep on top of the situation. 'No one is being forced to do anything,' he said, holding his hands up defensively. 'This has to be your decision.'

'You've got to give them something,' a soft Scottish voice protested.

Alice added her commentary. 'Do you know John Tay? He's directing the play and has done an excellent job too. He and Katherine have worked together many times before; they're very close.'

Bertie nodded.

On the stage, the director continued. 'To ask a cast of actors to perform in these conditions, you've got to give some proper reassurance, something with some substance, not just hollow words.'

'We have brought in every member of staff we have,' the theatre manager explained. 'There will be extra ushers lining the sides of auditorium and we have extra carpenters and crew to keep an eye out backstage.'

'What about the police?' came a strong female voice. 'Will the police be present?' The voice belonged to Katherine Debenham, who walked calmly to the front of the group until she was facing the theatre manager directly. Around her, bodies moved out of the way to automatically make space for her; the air around leading performers always feels a little denser.

'Mrs Debenham, there will be a small police presence. At least there will be *one* policeman present. As I said, they don't consider this to be a serious risk, although we're inclined to take a different view on the matter, especially with the emergence of this note that arrived today reiterating the threat.' He looked over Katherine's shoulder, addressing the rest of the group behind her. 'I can't impress on you enough how this really is your choice; none of you have to perform today if you don't feel comfortable. We can cancel and I will back you in that decision, if that's what you all think is best.'

Katherine spun around to address the group herself. 'Nonsense. Personally, I don't see that there is an issue. It's our last matinee and I rather suspect that someone is playing a bad-humoured practical joke on us. Now, we can either stand around talking about this some more or we can get on with things as usual. If we wait any longer, we'll be doing everything in a rush and I don't think that will be good for any of us or for the show. I, for one, am going to go and start getting ready. I strongly urge that you all do the same.'

With her final words spoken, Katherine strode through the centre of the group, leaving nothing in her wake apart from a few bemused faces. The other actors remained rooted to the spot, letting her pass in stony silence. Once she had disappeared from view, the people that were dotted around the stage seemed to snap out of the kind of daze they had fallen into. It seemed as if Katherine had said the last word on the matter and the meeting was over.

Bertie and Alice looked at each other. 'Well, at least she seems to have her mind made up,' he said.

'Come on,' she said, encouraging him to follow her. She led him a little further down the aisle and through a door at the side of the auditorium. After travelling down some more stairs and a long winding corridor, they emerged on to the stage.

As they arrived, Bertie noticed that the crowd had thinned a little more. Some had followed Katherine's lead and headed backstage so they could start getting ready for the show. Several of the others had remained on the stage talking animatedly with each other in hushed, frantic tones. John was deep in conversation with the theatre manager but broke off when he saw Bertie and Alice approach.

'Two playwrights in the same theatre?' he said in mock astonishment. 'I never thought I'd see the day.'

Bertie gave a small smile. 'Unlikely, perhaps, but not entirely unheard of. Alice asked me to come down, to see if there was anything I could do. I'm not sure there is; you seem to have everything under control.'

'Oh, I wouldn't say that,' John interjected. If he had intended the comment to be a light-hearted response, he hadn't quite managed it. Instead, he sounded rather nervous.

'I suppose you could think of me as some sort of mascot...' Bertie suggested.

The director nodded in return. 'Our lucky charm.'

'I'm very happy to be here.' Bertie turned to Alice, placing a comforting hand on her shoulder. 'For moral support, of course.'

John sighed. 'I suppose our luck was due to run out. This place has been in the depths for quite some time. Nothing seems to last here. Well, we thought we might have turned a corner with this one, being such a hit. Against the reputation of this theatre, we've actually made it as far as the last day in the run. We've got the draw of a great husband-and-wife team, not to mention the star draw of our playwright and a brilliant play. Until today, we were doing rather good business, all things considered.'

Bertie nodded in agreement. 'Full houses?'

'Not quite, but not at all bad. Ticket sales only seem to have improved since that advert appeared in the newspaper. Word has got out about it and audience numbers have shot up. The last few days, and of course the matinee performance today, have all been completely full.'

Alice spoke with a solemn expression, shaking her

head. 'You can write a good play, but you can't compete with the draw of a blood sport.'

'Should have thought of it myself,' said the director. 'A stunt like that to pull in the crowds.'

'That's what you think it is, then? A stunt?' Bertie shifted his gaze between the pair of them.

'Until the anonymous note arrived today, then yes, I'm afraid I did think that. Now?' The director left the question hanging, unanswered.

Bertie attempted to settle them all. 'You can't seriously expect someone to commit murder in the centre of the stage, during a live performance, can you?' With sudden realisation, his face fell.

John looked at the expression on Bertie's face and sighed. 'I suppose a few months ago I would have agreed with you. But then, after what happened with you in Brighton?'

Bertie was left speechless. A star, shot on stage, in front of a theatre audience... That was exactly what had happened.

Chapter Three

3

The few remaining cast members departed to their dressing rooms and the stage crew drifted off into the wings, not quite knowing what to do with themselves. They set about their work in an almost mechanical fashion, automatically, as they had done so many times before. The actors would get dressed, the props would be set and scenery arranged ready for the start of show. Everyone was intent on the pre-show routine remaining as normal as possible, despite everything. A comfort, in a way. As the actors left the stage, they shuffled past Alice and Bertie; some gave a brief nod of recognition, but many drifted by in their own world, distracted.

Alice and Bertie tried their best to rearrange their features into the semblance of a smile and to conjure up some kind words of reassurance, but they felt hopelessly ill-equipped to provide any level of comfort. Conversely, the two of them had begun to feel quite useless. But as writers, words were all they had to give.

Anthony Debenham was among the last of the actors to leave the stage. He caught sight of the newly arrived playwright as he moved towards the exit. 'Bertie! It's wonderful to see you; it must have been years. I'm only sorry it's under such unusual circumstances.' He spoke with a warmth of tone and smile that didn't quite reach his eyes.

'Anything I can do?' Bertie offered. 'I guess I'm here as a bit of a—'

'A good-luck charm?' Anthony scoffed loudly. 'Not likely. Murder and theatre seem to be following you around at the moment.' He gave Bertie a hearty slap on the back, accompanied by an equally hearty laugh.

Alice's face fell. 'Oh no, what have I done? I thought you'd be able to help, a reassuring presence. Now, I wonder if I've doomed us even further.'

'Well, thanks Alice, that really makes me feel great,' said Bertie, only half joking. 'Of course, you were only doing what you thought was right.'

'No,' added Anthony, his face becoming more serious. 'You are right, Alice, it's just me trying to lighten the mood in my own ham-fisted way. I don't know... I've performed under some bizarre and awkward circumstances in my career. Badly behaved audiences, half-empty houses, children, animals... Nothing like this, though. This is quite fantastic, like something from out of

The Phantom of the Opera.'

For a moment, and almost automatically, his eyes flitted up to the large chandelier that hung above the empty seats awaiting their audience. Bertie and Alice's attention was drawn in the same direction too. The delicate little pieces of cut glass looked quite perilous, hung and draped from the elaborate and intricate metalwork. The whole thing came together at the top, where it was suspended by a single, central point.

Anthony resumed talking, thankfully diverting their attention back down to the stage. 'It really is quite horrific. Although, I'm sure as soon as we start the performance, we'll all slip naturally back into our usual roles. In a way it becomes something of a habit once you've done it so many times. But right now, it feels like we're performing in some kind of real-life gothic horror.'

He shook his head gently as he walked away, leaving his ominous words hanging over them. He left the stage and disappeared through the door that led to the dressing rooms.

Alice looked at Bertie, a pained expression on her face. 'I did do the correct thing asking you here, didn't I?'

'In this situation, I don't think there is a *correct* thing to do. Come on,' said Bertie, with more enthusiasm. 'I've not been backstage at this theatre before, so let's go for a nose around.'

Alice guided him through a door that led away from the side of the stage and into the corridor. They came immediately face to face with a door to one of the dressing rooms. There were not the usual numbers, which would have been screwed or painted onto the plain white door, just a small, brightly polished brass holder with a slip of card that indicated the occupants.

When Bertie read the people listed, he was surprised to see that there were several names written up, not just the single one of the star performer. 'Katherine's not taken the principal dressing room?'

'Oh yes, the drama with the dressing rooms.' Alice rolled her eyes. 'Too close to the stage door, too many people trundling past on their way in and out, apparently. Gareth – or is it James – the theatre manager, tried to explain that it was only because the fit-up was still going on. Of course, it would only be natural there would be some disturbance while all the props, costumes and set were being loaded in. It would quieten down a bit when things got settled and rehearsals were properly underway.'

'That didn't reassure her?'

She shrugged. 'No, she wouldn't have it, so she moved to the floor above – much quieter. Had to bump her old husband out of his room to make space for her, which he wasn't particularly happy about. They agreed to let the three girls in the supporting roles share this one instead, which was incredibly generous of them. They have several costume changes to make during the play, so that does make things easier for everybody. There is a poky little lift, so it's not like our leads have to trudge up and down. It's all very modern, completely automatic.'

'Yes, very convenient,' said Bertie.

Alice led the way. 'You'd hate it. I know you're not a fan of small spaces, so we can take the stairs instead, if you want.'

Bertie was thankful for that. While his claustrophobia was only mild and he was happy to take larger lifts, like the one he'd ridden at the Underground station, he would still avoid smaller enclosed spaces whenever he could. While an automatic lift seemed state of the art, he didn't like the idea of being stuck in a tiny lift without an attendant around as a reassuring presence.

They climbed the steps heading to the next floor where the other dressing rooms were located. As they did, they heard a light knocking. 'Half hour, miss,' came a young man's voice.

Rounding the corner, they saw a small boy standing there – perhaps thirteen or fourteen – in a green uniform, immaculately pressed, with a neat cap perched on his head. He was so smartly turned out he could have been a bellboy from one of the nearby hotels on the Strand.

He knocked again. 'Miss?'

'No one in?' asked Bertie, slightly concerned.

'She'll be in Mr Debenham's room, most likely. Sir, miss,' the boy addressed each of them separately with a nod before turning and setting off on his way, heading up the stairs.

'Twenty years and still as in love as ever, those two. Can't bear to be apart. Can you imagine that?' said Alice in amazement. 'To be frank, I'm not sure I could stay fond of anything after twenty years.'

'No marriage proposals on the horizon for you then?'

She laughed. 'At my age? I should think not. I'm what people call "fiercely independent". For some reason they always say it in a tone of voice that sounds disapproving. Let us just say, I'm incompatible with that sort of life. Suggest to any man that you want to continue a playwriting career rather than turn housewife, they'll look at you like you've got a screw loose.'

'I can quite imagine,' said Bertie.

The pair of them followed after the speedy call boy as he dashed up to the next floor. As they ascended the last few steps, they could already hear his voice emanating through the dressing room door that was ajar. 'There is a guest at the stage door asking for—'

'Not now,' Anthony interrupted. 'Haven't we got enough on already?'

'Yes, sir,' the young voice politely replied. 'Sir, miss.' Once again, he addressed each of them in turn before emerging back into the corridor.

As he caught sight of Bertie and Alice a wide grin spread across his face. 'What did I tell you about Mrs Debenham? You want to know where anyone is in this place, ask for me – Dennis!' he said with a smile, giving a cheeky wink. He zipped off to carry out the rest of his duties.

'Honestly, it's exhausting just watching him run around like that,' said Bertie.

'Thankfully we're not reliant on you to make sure everyone is called down to the stage on time. Come through here.' With a mischievous look, Alice pointed to a door that had a sign marked *No Unauthorised Access*.

'Are you sure?'

'Oh absolutely. It's terrifying,' she said with a smile and disappeared through it. Bertie had no alternative but to follow her.

Alice's choice of words had been correct: they emerged onto a long platform that jutted out from one of the theatre's internal walls. The thin gantry ran the full depth of the stage. Gingerly peering over the side, they could see the scenery and the stage floor a long way below them. Above them, a yawning void was capped by hundreds of wooden beams, with gaps between large enough for the ropes that suspended the scenery and lighting equipment to dangle through them.

Rows of battens, with lights glowing in them, lit the stage. They were hanging almost level with where they stood. It was close enough for Bertie to feel the warmth coming from them and smell the dust burning off in the heat where it had settled on top.

Looking at the tangled web of ropes and knots, Bertie wondered if he would ever step on a stage again without feeling nervous about all the equipment that was dangling precariously above him. His head suddenly felt very soft and delicate.

'Welcome to the fly floor,' Alice announced, grandly.

As his eyes were drawn down its full length, he was met with a new terrifying sight. One man stood on top of the chunky wooden railing that ran along the fly floor, holding on to a clump of three ropes that descended from above. He had a flat cap on and his sleeves rolled up, ready for action. He was peering down towards the stage, patiently waiting for his signal. While he did, he lazily puffed on a cigarette without a care in the world – as if he wasn't inches away from falling to a certain death. With a slight change of costume, Bertie could picture him as a pirate, standing on the gunwale of a ship looking out to sea.

Receiving the signal, the man nodded to two others standing beneath him on the fly floor, also waiting and ready. Together they hauled the set of ropes at a tremendous speed, shooting the scenery it was attached to up into the rafters until the bottom was level with them. In a swift, practised sequence of movements, the man standing above held on to the bundle of ropes, while a second below quickly looped and tied them off to a large cleat fixed to the wooden rail. The third coiled the excess rope that had piled up on the floor and hung it neatly on top. It was done with the kind of swift, relaxed professionalism that came with doing the same thing a hundred times before.

Catching sight of the two new visitors, the man jumped down in a positively swashbuckling way and approached them with a smile. 'Alright, Alice. What brings you up here?'

'Today I've brought a friend. Bertie, this is Sam – we've become very good friends,' she explained.

Sam took a few steps closer, with a definite twinkle in

his eye, and offered his hand in greeting, which Bertie shook. His grip was strong, his skin slightly rough by the nature of his work. 'Nice to meet you, Bertie,' he said, still a touch breathless from the display of athleticism. There was a slight redness to his cheeks and Bertie realised that he found that the resulting effect was not entirely unattractive.

'This was my place of solace when I needed to disappear during rehearsals and wanted to avoid any more questions from the director or the actors,' said Alice. 'Sam has been very good at keeping my visits a secret. I'm not exactly an "authorised person" and the warning sign was very clear.'

'Oh yes.' He gave a knowing look at Bertie then added, 'I'm very good at keeping secrets, aren't I?' The wink he added in Alice's direction was not required. The subtext was clear – Alice, quite predictably, had been gossiping again.

Bertie felt a little embarrassed but smiled politely. There was not a lot you could get past a flyman. From their position high above everyone else, largely unnoticed, they saw everything.

'He's even been helping me out, you know. You gave me a great idea for a line at the end of the second act, didn't you?' She spoke of him as if she was a proud mother.

Sam took a final draw on his cigarette before stubbing it out in a nearby fire bucket. The metal bucket, which hung on the wall, contained not only sand but a mounting number of cigarette butts, too. 'You know, if you ever need any help with *your* plays, Mr Carroll, I'd be happy to oblige.'

Bertie smiled politely. 'I'll bear that in mind.'

'Just go and hang out near the theatre where his next play is on,' said Alice. 'You'll know he needs help when you see him doing laps around the block.'

'What can I say?' said Bertie. 'I think on my feet.'

A shout floated up from someone down on the stage. 'House open!'

Bertie glanced at his wristwatch. 'Alice, is that the time? I should go and get a seat.'

Sam retreated back down the fly floor, giving a cheeky salute as farewell, joining the other men, who had been completely uninterested in the visitors.

Bertie leaned in closely, talking in a hushed voice. He didn't appreciate the attempt at matchmaking. 'Alice, if you're trying to—'

She cut him off with a wave of her hand. 'Bertie,' she said, looking serious, 'it's just my way of taking my mind off things. I'm absolutely sure something terrible is going to happen. Would you begrudge a girl for trying to help out a friend and his love life?'

'My love life does not need any help and, certainly, it is none of your responsibility,' he protested lightly as they bundled their way back out through the small door.

'Well, someone's got to take responsibility for it. You don't seem to be progressing it very far.'

'With your track record in partners? I don't think I'll be taking any lessons from you!'

Their bickering continued all the way to Bertie's seat.

Chapter Four

4

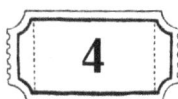

Bertie shuffled his chair into the corner of the box at the side of the auditorium. It was a somewhat futile attempt to get a better view of the stage. When the curtain rose, anything that took place to his left would be out of his sight.

Like most theatres, the horseshoe shape of the auditorium meant that the audience's view of the people sitting *in* the box was much better than the view of the stage *from* the box. For that reason, Bertie tended to avoid the exposing seats in this position. He'd much rather sit among the audience, preferring to blend in and stay hidden.

Perhaps the Victorian and Edwardian theatregoers would have felt quite the opposite to Bertie if they had been sitting in the same place when the Gaiety had been at the height of its powers. Maybe they would have relished the idea of putting themselves on display and showing off.

He had only ended up in this unfortunate position because every other seat had already been sold. The box, which was always kept reserved for the use of the director or the theatre managers, was the only place left for him to sit.

As soon as Alice had deposited him there, she turned, determined to leave the box before the show started. 'I don't know how you can bear to watch your own shows, Bertie. All I do is sit there, listening, and thinking endlessly about the far more interesting words I could have used instead.'

She hovered for a moment with one hand on the door, as if she was braced to make a dash for it in case the curtain started to rise. 'Bertie,' she said, her voice sounding a little ominous. 'Thank you for doing this for me.'

Bertie gave her an encouraging look as she departed. At least, he gave what he hoped was an encouraging look. The anxiety of the upcoming performance, which was slowly building in him, meant he didn't quite have full control of his facial features.

There are plenty of directors and writers who can't bear to watch their own show with an audience, especially on an opening night. They only sneak in for the curtain call, trying to judge the success of the evening from the audience's reaction as the cast take their bows.

Whatever this nervous disposition was, Bertie didn't

seem to have it. He was quite happy to watch his shows with an analytical eye. It often meant that he would be commandeered to report back on his own first nights by a nervous director or theatre manager. Instead, they would wait in the front-of-house bar or sometimes even a drinking establishment across the road from the theatre. Rather than be able to take a relaxing break from proceedings during the intervals on an opening night, he would arrive to be grilled by the awaiting group who were eager to see how the play was being received.

Bertie had always had a habit of seeking out productions of his own plays, something he tried to keep a secret – although there were some, like Alice, who did know. To him, it was less an exercise in egotism and more a way to keep him humble – not that he needed the extra help in that regard. Watching previous plays, hearing how the audiences responded to the lines, and how that reaction subtly changed over the years, allowed him to continually learn from his plays. It meant he could tweak the current ones he was working on, making sure they stayed relevant. At their very best, plays could challenge an audience, sway opinion, provoke thoughts. There were also some times when you just needed to give the audience what they wanted and his success proved that Bertie was able to do that year after year.

Unfortunately, it was this habit that led him to be in Brighton six months ago and ending up being an unwitting witness to a murder. Now he sat with his fingers firmly crossed and desperately hoped that history wasn't about to repeat itself.

Today, he was thankful for his position in the box. It allowed him to cast his eye around the auditorium and see the gathering audience members. The show was about to begin and the theatre was very nearly full. The few last stragglers made their way to their seats. There was an excitable buzz in the room. Every now and then Bertie would catch snippets of the different conversations, the words of which seemed to float around the place. 'Did you see in *The Era*...' '... a real murder?' There was no doubt as to why the atmosphere was more highly charged than usual. He felt the hairs on his arms rise a little. It was almost as if the chatter and excitement were bumping off each other, rubbing together and creating their own static electricity.

When the house lights finally dimmed and the curtain rose, a tense hush descended over the entire auditorium. Some of the people in the audience leaned forward in their seats in anticipation. Bertie felt uncomfortable. Would someone really try to commit a murder during the matinee performance? Even though the director had been right and that was exactly what had happened at the Palace Pier Theatre, no one had been expecting that to happen in advance – in fact everyone who had been watching was quite unaware that a murder had even taken place. Here, both the audience and everyone involved in the production were pre-warned; they were alert and vigilant. It would be complete madness for someone to attempt something that audacious.

Bertie's attention was drawn by the movement of several ushers in uniform, as well as other members of the theatre's staff, who had been brought in especially and were patrolling the aisles. As they crept quietly in the dark, they kept an eye out for anything unusual in the crowd. Despite Alice's protestations that the police were hopeless and the theatre manager had said they were only expecting one constable to be present, Bertie could see at least two uniformed officers hovering at the side of the room and wondered if there were more stationed around the building. Maybe Gareth had thought that by playing down the size of the police presence, he might also play down the size of the threat in front of the actors.

With all the extra goings-on, Bertie found it difficult to take his eyes off the packed auditorium. It was lit by the reflected glow of the light falling from the stage. Distracted, he ended up missing most of the opening of the play, but as time moved on, he found that he was able to relax enough to start taking it in. As the play marched on, without any incident, the audience seemed to become less tense as well.

It was what you might call a domestic thriller and an acting tour de force by the two leading actors. The play revolved around a husband and wife who seemed to loathe each other and were each secretly plotting the other's death. They were both very convincing at portraying their characters – quite a stretch, as their feelings for each other in real life were clearly the polar opposite.

The first act seemed to pass by without any incident

and when the curtain fell on the second, Bertie went to join Alice, who was nervously waiting in the upstairs bar. He made his way through the mass of bodies that were gathered there, chatting excitedly, and found her sitting on a stool in the corner.

Her face brightened when she saw Bertie approach. 'Oh, thank goodness. I don't know how much more of this I can bear. Gareth has said that I can go and sit in his office and be plied with brandy for the rest of the show, until this is all over.'

'Maybe he's right. I don't think you should be alone. I can always stay with you, if you would like?'

'No, you should stay in there. You should watch it. Besides, I could always take some of your advice. You might have some good ideas for changes if it goes on tour. I know you always give the best suggestions when it comes to that sort of thing.'

'To be honest, Alice, I'm paying very little attention to the play. I'm somewhat distracted. We all are.' He gestured to the other audience members in the bar who were talking animatedly among themselves.

Alice looked around the room, a worried expression on her face. The first two acts of the show had passed by without incident, but the mood was quickly changing as they approached the third.

'I don't know what we were thinking, Bertie. We should have cancelled the show instead. You know, better safe than sorry.'

'I think I agree. The atmosphere is beginning to build

34

to quite a fever pitch in there. I'm just hoping that ev.
one leaves disappointed.'

In the distance a bell could be heard ringing.

'I suppose I'd better get back to my seat,' said Bertie.
His words were tinged with a strong sense of
apprehension. 'Go to the theatre manager's office, stay
there, stay safe. Either way, whatever happens, this will all
be over soon.' He placed a comforting hand on her
shoulder.

Alice drained the last of her drink and put the glass on
the small shelf that ran around the room. 'Yes, you're
right. I'll see you when it's all over.'

Before leaving, she gave him the strongest bear hug he
had ever received and disappeared into the crowd. He
filtered out of the bar with the remaining audience members and back to his seat.

This was it. The words of the advert floated to the
front of his mind: *A terrifying and very real murder will
be committed in the third act.*

This time, when the curtain rose, a deathly quiet
descended across the room. It was not just silent, but
somehow more than silent, as if all the air had been
sucked from the room. It felt like everyone who was
watching had breathed in, but not a single person had
dared breathe out again.

The finale of the play was a stunning anti-climax.
Neither of the married pair seemed to be able to pull off
their intended killing of each other and they seemed
destined for endless purgatory together as the curtain fell.

nd of the play was met with well-deserved
e, although there was much whispering and
ing between the audience members throughout the
curtain call. Everyone's thoughts turned from the play to
the advert, wondering whether it really had just been a
promotional tactic or a practical joke.

The murder that was promised in the advert seemed
to have mirrored the plot of the play and not taken place.
There were no screams, no calls for help, no dramatic
deaths on the stage. Was it the additional presence of
theatre staff and police officers that had dissuaded the
murderer from going through with it?

The very moment the house lights came up, Bertie
dashed along the winding route from the box that led to
the backstage areas, heading to the theatre manager's
office on the top floor. If he wanted confirmation that
nothing untoward had happened behind the scenes as
well, that was where he would find it.

As he passed by the dressing rooms, spirits seemed to
be high, which was already a good sign. As he passed by
Anthony Debenham's dressing room, the door swung
open causing him to jump.

'Oh, sorry Bertie. Didn't mean to startle you,'
Anthony said. He directed his attention to the stairwell
and shouted loudly down it. 'Have you got glasses down
there, darling?'

Katherine's voice echoed back up in reply. 'Yes.'

'Deserves a glass of champagne, don't you think?' he
said to Bertie, then he shouted down the staircase, 'Be there

in a moment!'

'Nothing went wrong then?' asked Bertie.

'The whole thing went off without a hitch.' Anthony smiled broadly, before disappearing back into his room, the door closing behind him with a loud slam. Head down, Bertie set off up the next set of stairs at a jog.

'Whoa,' came a familiar voice. Bertie only just managed to stop himself crashing into a man on the stairs. 'Someone's in a hurry,' said Sam, straightening his flat cap.

'Sorry, just anxious to get up to Alice and the others. All I want to know is that everything went smoothly. How were things from up where you are?'

Sam smiled. 'From where I am, everything looks great.'

'I'd better—'

'Go, go.' Sam encouraged Bertie onwards, giving a chuckle as he shot past.

Bertie had finally made it to the top floor and the door to the office was ajar. He slipped inside to find that Gareth James, the theatre manager, John Tay, the director, and Alice were all gathered there.

He was a little out of breath after the long climb and his words tumbled out a little more dramatically that he had intended. 'It's all alright? Nothing happened?'

'Nothing happened,' confirmed the Scottish director, looking relieved.

Bertie smiled through heavy breaths. 'Thank God for that.'

Alice, her nervousness now melted away, returned his smile from across the room. 'I think we should go for a bite of something, don't you? I've just realised, I haven't been able to eat a thing all day and now I'm absolutely ravenous!'

Chapter Five

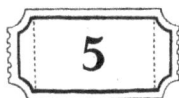

If you were seeing a show down by the Gaiety Theatre, there was really only one place you could go to dine: Romano's. The history of these two places was inextricably linked, although as the years went past, it was becoming more and more difficult to tell fact from fiction as people told and retold their tales. With each repeat of the same timeworn stories, more outlandish and exaggerated embellishments seemed to develop.

Was it true that in the past, gentlemen would drink champagne from the slippers of the beautiful Gaiety girls? No one was really sure. Certainly, it was true that some of the girls had gone on to marry earls, barons or marquesses. The situation was further complicated as no one could agree if the owner's heavy Italian accent had been real or if he had been putting it on the entire time.

"The Roman", as he was known, had long since passed away. With him, some of the spirit of the place had died too.

No longer was this a place where artists, gamblers, crooks and – on the odd occasion – even royalty would mingle together. The people that still dined here did so partly out of loyalty, but mainly out of habit. When you were in this part of London, coming here was the easy choice to make. You would be quite likely to recognise a friendly face or two, even if the names would escape you. Theatre folk and journalists would still hang about, in case a scrap of information could be overheard. Here you still might be able to pick up a hint about a new job or some titbit for a gossip column. It wasn't hard to do so: the customers were crammed in elbow to elbow. They always had been.

The restaurant was buzzing with chatter. The combination of the post-matinee crowd and those who were dining before they caught an evening performance created a continual low murmur, which was occasionally punctuated by the sharp sound of cutlery clattering on plates. Alice, who had completely lost her appetite due to nerves, hadn't eaten all morning. She spent a considerable amount of time trying to decide what it was she wanted, was unable to make a decision and seemed to have ordered half the menu instead. Bertie looked down in front of him, where you could barely see the tabletop for plates – the number of which were rapidly growing.

'Are you sure you've got enough, Bertie? Here, have

40

another potato,' she said. Without waiting for him to answer she sent one sailing over in his direction; it landed on his plate with a thud. 'Now we've got all of that dreadful business out of the way, you can tell me everything that's going on. I hope you got that awful review I sent you?'

He smiled wryly and nodded. 'Yes, that one was particularly terrible.' In recent years Alice and Bertie had got into the habit of sending each other the worst review they could find of each other's productions. The more appalling, the better. The one she had sent was a particularly nasty review of one of Bertie's touring productions, something she had managed to track down in some local newspaper or other. He supposed it was one way of making sure that success wouldn't go to their heads.

'What's the story with your new play? I assume it's going to be another box office smash?' Alice gestured with her fork as she spoke.

'Well, we'll see about that. We're yet to find a theatre that will take us – we're not doing too well on that front. At the moment we've been given a choice between the Winter Garden and the Ambassadors.'

Alice failed in her attempt to hold in her laugher. 'But those are such entirely different places. The Winter Garden is a huge barn of a place and the Ambassadors is the size of a postage stamp.'

'Well, yes,' agreed Bertie. 'Ideally what we need is somewhere in between the two, but nowhere else seems

41

forthcoming right now. It's sad that we can't hold on to the Garrick, where my production of *Witnessed* is currently playing. Something else is booked to go in there. It's not you, is it?'

Alice shook her head. 'It's not one of mine, although that play of yours has done rather well there, hasn't it? Too big, too small… Finding a place that's the right size is the trick, isn't it? Mind you, I'd much rather it be too small than too big. At least you can extend the show for a few weeks if you need to. Nothing worse than a half-empty theatre, especially when it's the size of the Winter Garden.'

'Yes, but as I keep getting reminded, you need to sell every single ticket in a smaller theatre if you want to make sure you cover the costs. It seems as if those are the only discussions I have these days. Everything is about costs, salaries and ticket prices. Never any talk about the actual play, of course, which I'm still not completely happy with. I'm terribly worried that it might not be good enough to draw people in, even in a small venue like the Ambassadors.'

Alice let her fork clatter down and leaned back in her chair. 'Absolute rubbish. You're a very good writer and you know it's true because *I'm* the one who's saying it. Yes, very good – not quite as good as me, of course,' she added with a twinkle in her eye.

Bertie sighed. 'I wish I had your self-confidence.'

'I wish I had your modesty.' Alice laughed. 'Apparently, I don't go down well with some people. Can you believe that!'

Bertie smiled, raising his eyebrows. 'I had heard.'

Before he could continue talking, his eye was caught by someone in a large coat being led to a table by a waiter. A little oversized for the weather, the plush fabric brushed against Alice as the figure walked past. Alice turned, annoyed, but the feeling faded immediately when she recognised the person as Katherine Debenham.

'That's funny,' she said. 'I thought she left before we did.'

Following behind Katherine was another person, which came as something of a surprise to Bertie.

'Margo Murray?' He looked back at Alice. 'Well, that's a turn up for the books, don't you think? I thought they were sworn enemies.'

'I thought *we* were sworn enemies?' Alice said, with a smile, raising a glass in a mock toast.

Bertie watched them arrive at their table where they were handed menus by an exhausted-looking waiter.

'Yes, I know that technically we're supposed to be. But we're rivals in a very friendly way, not like them. Some of the things she's written, the kinds of reviews she's given to Katherine over the years... I'm surprised that she'd give her the time of day, let alone sit down to eat with her.'

Alice seemed less interested in the goings-on across the room and returned her attention to the remaining food on their table. 'Well, sometimes you have to let these things go. Let bygones be bygones and all that. You can't be on the wrong side of the press forever. It's a smart idea, taking out a journalist for dinner. Maybe you can change their opinion of you.'

Bertie looked back over at the unlikely couple. Margo was sitting with her arms folded, looking unimpressed. 'In their case, I think that would take some doing,' he commented.

'I'm surprised she left her husband behind at the theatre, mind you. They've been inseparable the whole time. I suppose it's one of those business things, isn't it? She's always been the one that deals with that side of their lives.'

'The two of them, the perfect team. Inseparable. That's what the call boy said, wasn't it?'

'Oh, yes,' said Alice, impressed. 'They're always acting like young lovebirds. I imagine if I'd been married for twenty years, I would have got quite bored of that sort of thing by now. I suppose that says more about me than it does them.'

'So, no weddings on the horizon for you then?'

Her eyes sparkled. 'I promise you, Bertie, I'll get married the very next day after you.'

He laughed; now it was his turn to raise his glass in a toast. 'Deal.'

She turned in her chair, looking behind her and leaning over so she could get a clear view of them.

Bertie rolled his eyes. 'Yes, that's right, keep it subtle.'

'Politeness is overrated if you ask me,' she joked, observing the odd pairing through squinted eyes. 'What do you think they're talking about?'

'I honestly have no idea.'

'You know, she actually gave our show a good review,' Alice said, turning back to face Bertie. 'Maybe that acid tongue of hers is losing its sting, not that Mrs Debenham was mentioned in it particularly. Maybe that's a sign that their old rift is over. Getting no notice is better than a bad notice, I suppose.'

'I hate reading about myself. I'd be perfectly happy with receiving no notice,' commented Bertie.

'Yes, well *you* would be.'

'If I had to talk face to face with a journalist like that, I'm positive that I'd say something wrong and that would make everything ten times worse,' he admitted.

Alice let out a short, sharp laugh. 'I don't mind telling you that I've put my foot in it on more than one occasion; it doesn't seem to have harmed me. We must really work on your shyness, you know. After all, I am talking to the man who missed one of his own opening nights because the people on the door failed to recognise him and wouldn't let him in... All because you were too polite to mention that you were, in fact, the playwright.'

Bertie looked at her sheepishly. 'Yes, but it was only for half an hour. The producer came outside to rescue me when he eventually noticed I was missing.'

Alice took another glance over at the table across the room. 'Well, neither of them seems to have a problem with being too polite.'

Bertie looked over to see what she meant. She was

right. The two of them were now both leaning over the table in an adversarial way, deep in an intense exchange. He let his eyes wander around the room. Most of the people sitting at the other tables were engaged in relaxed conversation. Some were talking in hushed tones, quite seriously. Others were enjoying themselves much more, laughing loudly. There were a few faces mixed among the crowd that he recognised. Some were friendly faces he knew from previous shows, others known just by reputation.

That was the problem with working in an industry where you meet new people all the time, work with them intensely for a few weeks and then move on again. You would often recognise faces, but not always be able to put a name to them. For example, he recognised the man sitting alone just behind Katherine Debenham's table, but couldn't quite place him. No wonder those that worked in the theatrical world would resort to calling people "darling" or "dear". In an industry where people traded on their names, it would be much worse to admit that you'd forgotten it altogether.

As his eyes reached the entrance, he came across a sight that was entirely unexpected – the broad frame of a man who he instantly recognised. At the sight of him, he felt a surge of excitement – a kind of lightness and happiness that he hadn't felt in months – but it rapidly subsided. Detective Chief Inspector Hugh Chapman, and Bertie's old school friend, had entered Romano's. And that could only mean one thing.

Hugh made swift progress across the restaurant, led by one of the waiters. Bertie watched intently, his eyes fixed on the detective, almost as if willpower alone would cause him to turn in their direction and notice them.

He didn't turn to see Bertie or Alice, continuing directly past their table. Bertie's heart sank; surely there was only one place that Hugh could be heading. In the direction of Katherine Debenham. His face fell. 'Oh no.'

'What is it?' asked Alice, who hadn't yet realised what the change in his mood or significance of the newly arrived figure meant. She glanced over at the table, then back at Bertie, looking for some sort of explanation.

'That's Hugh. You know... From Scotland Yard.'

'Your detective?'

'He's not *my* detective,' Bertie said. 'But yes.'

They were not the only people to notice something was amiss, as heads began to turn at every table to try and see what was going on. Hugh was leaning down and talking with Mrs Debenham as discreetly as he could manage. Bertie watched, unable to hear what was going on, but the pained expression on the actress's face explained everything.

A second policeman, who had accompanied Hugh, put out an arm to help Mrs Debenham to her feet. However, she ignored the offer of assistance and rose unaided before striding from the room without another word. The policeman followed in close pursuit.

Back at the table, Margo Murray was left with nothing to do but sit with her mouth open. Behind her, the young man Bertie had recognised earlier was watching the goings-on carefully. From the confused expression he could see on the man's face, he seemed to be trying to work out what on earth what had happened, just like everyone else in the restaurant.

As Hugh turned to make his way to the exit, Bertie stood on impulse, catching his attention. Their eyes met briefly and for a moment it seemed as if Hugh would continue out of the restaurant without stopping to acknowledge him. A few steps from the entrance, he seemed to change his mind and diverted over towards Bertie and Alice instead.

When he arrived at the table, Bertie opened his mouth to speak but was quickly cut off.

'Bertie,' Hugh said. 'Sorry to interrupt your meal.' He nodded at Alice. 'I suppose it's Miss Crawford, isn't it? I'm afraid there's been an incident at the theatre. The body of Mr Debenham has been found—'

'Dead?' she interrupted, her mouth falling open in disbelief.

'I'm afraid so. I think it would be a good idea if you would come with me.' He turned, about to leave.

'Bertie should come too, shouldn't he?' asked Alice.

'If you would like him to accompany you, then yes, he can come too.'

Hugh gave one last look in Bertie's direction. As he did, Bertie noticed a thin cut that was still healing above his left eye. There was no more time to look or to ask him about it; Hugh quickly turned on his heels and swept out of the building without another word.

Bertie looked over the table to Alice, who was looking solemnly at the uneaten plates of food. The colour had completely drained from her face. It appeared that she'd lost her appetite again.

Chapter Six

6

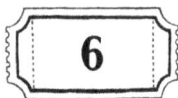

A small group of people with solemn faces had gathered in the theatre manager's office. The theatre manager himself sat behind a desk, sinking down in the chair with a grave look, ledgers and paperwork piled neatly around him. Hugh stood next to him, facing everyone who was gathered there, ready to address them.

One of the people who was standing across the room from him with a stony expression was Katherine Debenham. She had stoically refused a chair when it was offered to her. Instead, she was being supported by the director, John Tay, who had a comforting arm draped around her waist.

With one last look around the room, Hugh took a deep breath before he began. As he spoke, his eyes scanned the room, although he let them skip over Bertie, who stood next to Alice as her supporting presence.

'I'm afraid what you all feared has happened. There has been a murder here today. Anthony Debenham has been found, dead, in Mrs Debenham's dressing room.'

Katherine let out a pained cry. Unable to conjure up any comforting words in the moment, John drew her in a little closer.

'Mrs Debenham, I believe you were the last person to see him?'

'Alive,' she said, with a surprising forcefulness as she stepped forward into the centre of the room. 'I was the last person to see him *alive*. He left... Afterwards. He left the room...' Her words tailed away and she turned, collapsing back into the arms of the director.

'How was he killed?' said John, although he wasn't quite sure if it was appropriate to ask, especially as he was in such close proximity to the grieving wife.

'He was stabbed in the neck with a letter opener.' Hugh spoke in his usual matter-of-fact manner that he used to address a room full of people. It was a touch blunt, Bertie thought, causing Katherine to emit a loud cry, which was muffled by the director's chest as she turned into him.

'We are taking statements from everyone in the building but, naturally, there will be some people I will want to speak with individually. Mrs Debenham, I know that this is a difficult time, but I need to ask all of you some questions while the events are still fresh in your minds.'

Katherine turned to Hugh and nodded, once again standing up straight and away from the director a little. She was determined to answer on her own two feet.

'You said just now that Mr Debenham left your dressing room after the show?'

'Yes, that's correct. We had a drink, some champagne, to celebrate getting through the performance without any problems. Then he left, back to his own dressing room, I presumed.'

'You didn't dine together in between the shows?'

'No.'

'Isn't that unusual?'

'I had an engagement to meet for dinner with a journalist friend of mine, Margo Murray.'

'Would there have been any reason for him to return to your dressing room after you left?'

'I wouldn't have thought so, but he would often come down to my dressing room – it's quite possible he had left something in there he wanted to retrieve.'

'And what time did you leave, Mrs Debenham?'

'I met Margo at the stage door before we left for Romano's. We'd arranged to meet there at a quarter past five and he left my room just before I went down.'

'So, that means that he was killed somewhere between quarter past five and quarter to six, when he was discovered by one of the call boys. That's quite a tight window,' said Hugh, looking around the room. His eyes fell on the theatre manager, who seemed to snap out of a deep thought.

Gareth managed to mumble some kind of response. 'The evening show will have to cancelled, of course. I'll go round now and let everyone know.'

'We'll need to take full statements from everyone first and see if we can find anyone to corroborate this or narrow timings down further. Thank you, for now.'

He made a move to indicate that they were done and spoke more quietly to Katherine. 'I think perhaps you should wait here for now and only leave when you feel up to it. I have no more questions I need to ask at this time, but I may need to visit you again. You'll be at your home address?'

'Yes,' Katherine replied, shakily. 'Home... It will be so empty now.' She managed to hold herself together for only a few seconds before she broke down in tears again. At last, a few members of the group managed to persuade her to sit down in a chair.

As the others comforted her, Hugh discreetly left the room. No one seemed to notice apart from Bertie, who followed after him. Emerging into the corridor, Bertie closed the door gently.

'Hugh.'

Hugh had already made it halfway down the corridor, but hearing Bertie's voice he turned back.

Bertie approached. 'I haven't seen you for... How have you been?'

'Fine. I've been fine,' Hugh said, looking around the corridor awkwardly. 'I think you must realise this isn't exactly the best time.'

'I know,' said Bertie, gingerly. 'I just thought... I mean it's nice to see you again. If there's anything I can do to help.'

Hugh sighed. 'You can give your statement to one of my constables.'

'I will.'

'We can't...' Hugh began. 'We can't be together. What I mean is, you can't help out, not this time. This isn't like Brighton.'

'No,' said Bertie. *In more ways than one*, he thought.

'I'd better go,' said Hugh. He gave a small smile of consolation before turning and leaving the corridor.

Behind him, Bertie heard the door open and close. Alice joined him, looking down the corridor at the hurriedly departing Hugh.

'I thought I'd leave them to it,' she said with a nod in the direction of the office door. 'There's nothing worse, when you're feeling a bit delicate and vulnerable, to have a bunch of people crowding around you constantly asking how you are, is there?'

Bertie didn't reply.

'Everything alright?' she asked.

'I suppose it is.' Bertie turned back to face Alice. 'Now what?'

'I don't know, you're the one who's done this before. How do we go about solving a murder?'

He let out a laugh, smiling wryly. 'We're not going to solve this murder, Alice. Hugh's made it very clear that he's got everything in hand. We should just let them get on with it.'

Her face fell. 'Where's your sense of adventure? I bet we *could* solve it, you know. Why not let us prove to your inspector friend that he can't just brush you off, that he really does need you for these things.'

Bertie thought about it for a moment, but wasn't convinced.

Alice smiled. 'Besides, I've got a pile of important writing work that I should be doing instead, and this will be a wonderful distraction from having to do it.'

'I suppose a peek at what's going on couldn't hurt,' he said.

Together, they descended the stairs down to Katherine's dressing room. They stopped short of the last flight, making sure they stayed out of sight, hidden around the corner. Gingerly they poked their heads out so they had a clear line of sight down to the room's entrance.

Outside, it was guarded by two policemen, although the door was slightly ajar. Through the slim gap, they could just about make out the shapes of some people moving around but it was impossible to tell what else was going on inside.

'What's going on here?' came a voice from behind them.

They had been so focused on trying to interpret the scene in front of them that it made them both jump out of their skin. They turned around to see Dennis, the call boy that the two of them had met earlier in the day. He sat cheerily on the steps above them.

'You seem chipper?' commented Bertie.

'Oh, yes. Didn't you hear, I found a dead body and it was just awful.'

'*You* were the call boy that found the body?' Bertie was mildly amused and perhaps a little bit concerned for the young man's enthusiasm for the unpleasantness he had witnessed.

'I'm the *only* call boy. Do you want me to show you? I can show you what it looked like if you want?' he asked, eagerly.

'I don't think they'll allow us in Katherine's dressing room, you know,' said Bertie.

The call boy's eyes sparkled. 'Obviously not. What I mean is, I'll show you in one of the others, Mr Debenham's room, perhaps. There were some policemen in there poking around, but they finished looking a few minutes ago. I can show you exactly what it was like when I found him. Come on!'

Dennis set off up the stairs, with Bertie and Alice following closely behind as best they could; it was a struggle to keep up with his youthful enthusiasm. When they reached the next floor up, he led them towards Anthony Debenham's dressing room.

Opening the door, Dennis led them inside and spoke in a voice that you might usually reserve for telling ghost stories. 'Ooh, it was horrible it was. He was right there when I opened the door, face down on the floor. Couldn't miss him.' He eagerly lay down on the floor to demonstrate, his voice muffled as he spoke into the carpet.

'Like this, he was!'

Bertie took a cursory glance around the room, while Alice took a seat. 'That's a very accurate recreation. Thank you, Dennis. I think you ought to get up now. You don't want to ruin your uniform,' she said.

'Thanks, miss.' He leaped back to his feet and leaned casually against the dressing room table.

'It was definitely Mr Debenham?' asked Bertie.

'Oh yes.'

'Even though he was lying face down?'

'Well, he had the same clothes, the same coloured hair and it looked just like him, so I'm pretty sure. I ran off to get the manager right away. I suppose it was pretty dark in here with the curtains being closed, but you're not supposed to disturb the crime scene, are you? See, I know what I'm doing. I saw it once, in a play.' Dennis tapped the side of his nose, knowingly.

'But you didn't see his face?'

Dennis thought for a moment then shook his head. 'No, you're right, I didn't. Not that first time at least. What are you thinking? Someone could have switched the body? A Texas switch?'

'A what?' asked Alice, confused by the term.

'A Texas switch, like in the cowboy films. Don't you watch them?'

Alice shrugged her shoulders; she wasn't a regular cinema-goer.

'How it works is they get a body double to do the dangerous stunt – say someone getting thrown over the top of the counter in a bar room brawl, smashing all the glasses as they go. Once they've disappeared behind the counter and they're out of shot, the real actor pops up. It looks like he's done the whole thing.'

'Oh, well that's very clever,' she replied with a voice that did its best to sound as if she had grasped the concept.

'You mean, someone could have swapped the body while you were out of the room,' Bertie clarified.

Alice's eyes lit up, finally understanding. 'You mean, to disguise the time of the murder? It's a possibility, I suppose.'

'All possibilities, however unlikely, remain possible until they can be disproven.'

'Oh, that's very good Bertie,' said Alice, who sounded very impressed with his wise words. 'Is that something from one of your plays?'

Bertie smiled. 'From Hugh, actually. It was something he said to me last time. Although it *does* seem unlikely, doesn't it? I don't think anyone was moving bodies around, Dennis. I'm afraid there's not really much to go on, though I'm hardly an expert.'

'Now, don't be too hard on yourselves,' Alice said. 'I think you're both doing very well. You, with your possibilities, and Dennis here, with his Mexico switch idea, or whatever it was called.'

'Don't worry, Miss Crawford, we'll work out who it was in no time,' Dennis said happily, before turning to Bertie. 'Won't we, Mr Carroll... I bet you've nearly worked it out already?'

'I think it's a bit early for that,' said Bertie. He wandered to the other side of the room, picking up a copy of *Vogue* magazine that had been sitting on a table and began flicking through the pages. 'Presumably these weren't his?' he said, nodding to a pair of gloves that had been left next to it.

'Mrs Debenham's, most likely,' said Dennis. 'They were always in and out of each other's rooms. I'd often be sent up here to bring down something she'd left behind.'

Alice looked wistful. 'Can't keep away from each other for very long – that seems rather sweet, doesn't it? I think I'd find it a little tedious, if I'm being completely honest. I do have a heart of stone though...'

'Maybe you just need to find the right person,' Bertie commented over the top of the magazine, with a knowing smile. He dropped the publication back onto the table.

Alice chuckled. 'I think I've rather given up looking.' She turned her attention to Dennis. 'Why were you going into Katherine's dressing room when you came across Anthony?'

'Delivering the afternoon post. Mr James asks us to do it in between shows on matinee days. Often people are out so I just leave it on their dressing-room tables. I knocked, no one was in, and when I opened the door, there he was. Face down and that dagger thing in his neck. It was unbelievable, really. Just like something out of one of your plays.'

Chapter Seven

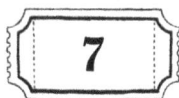

7

A feeling of concern hung over Bertie once they had let Dennis go on his way. The boy seemed content enough as he hopped down the stairs ahead of them and disappeared around the corner without a care. By the time he and Alice reached the bottom, Dennis, in his green uniform, was nowhere to be seen.

Alice turned to Bertie, thinking along the same lines. 'The capacity for children to deal with traumatic events is...'

'Startling?' he offered.

Alice nodded in agreement. 'It's funny, isn't it? You're able to tolerate all sorts of things as a youth that you'd never dream of doing as an adult. I seem to remember a particular obsession with frogspawn and newts as a young girl. I wouldn't go near any of that sort of stuff now.'

'Was that particularly traumatic?'

'It was if you'd have seen the state of our pond.'

As the pair of them chuckled lightly, they were approached by a policeman, which abruptly changed their mood. They were taken away to give their statements separately in one of the empty dressing rooms. If Bertie had hoped to have some time alone with Hugh while he answered questions, he was mistaken. A fresh-faced young constable diligently took down details of everything he could remember instead. Once he had listened to the policeman read everything back to him and confirmed there was nothing else he could add, Bertie was free to leave and hovered in the corridor waiting for Alice to finish. It took some time; clearly she had a lot more to say on the matter than he did.

Once she eventually emerged, the pair of them descended towards the stage door. As they went, they updated each other on the information they had given to the police. They slowed their pace and fell silent when they approached Katherine Debenham's dressing room. There was still a policeman on guard and the door had now been closed. As they walked past, Bertie strained to hear if there was any indication of detective work still going on behind the closed door. Alice moved a little awkwardly next to him; obviously she was doing the same thing.

They continued to sneak past, attempting to look as casual as they could. Bertie wondered why it was – even when you knew you hadn't done anything wrong – when you were in the presence of a policeman or figure of authority, you automatically began to act as if you were guilty of something. It seemed to take all his concentration to ensure that his limbs were properly coordinated as the pair of them walked awkwardly in front of the constable.

Once they were past the dressing room, they descended the final flight of stairs that led down towards the stage door. The greater the distance that they put between them and the policeman, the easier Bertie seemed to find the task of walking again. He smiled to himself: there was no way he'd ever make it as a career criminal.

Alice and Bertie gave a small wave of acknowledgement to the stage door keeper on their way out of the building. He gave nothing in return, absorbed in his newspaper.

When they emerged into the outside world, they looked gingerly around, unsure of what they should do next or where they should go. There was nothing left to do. The evening performance had, of course, been cancelled and the actors had filtered away. Around the front of the theatre, presumably tickets were being returned and refunds were being made, the box office staff having to break the tragic news to the arriving audience.

Something across the road caught Bertie's eye and he tapped Alice on the arm. He drew her attention to a female figure who seemed to be loitering nervously next to a tree. Just like the two of them, it seemed as if she didn't know what to do with herself.

The woman caught sight of Bertie looking in her direction and started gesticulating enthusiastically at them, inviting them to join her. Dodging the traffic, they managed to make it to the other side of the wide road.

'Hello, Margo,' said Alice coldly, as they arrived. 'Shouldn't you be busy somewhere, writing this all down?'

'Well, yes, although it's hard to know what to say.'

'That doesn't normally stop you,' Alice grumbled, unable to keep her opinions of the journalist to herself.

'I don't suppose you know what's going on?' Margo continued, pretending to ignore Alice's comment. 'I haven't been able to get much out of the police, although they wanted to question me. Can you believe that? I spent what felt like ages answering all sorts of questions for them. When they were finished, I was hoping I could get some sort of information out of one of them, you know. They wouldn't give me anything at all.'

'Oh, how the tables have turned.' Alice folded her arms. 'Well, that's just tough. I'm sorry to inform you that I don't engage in gossip.'

Bertie had to stifle a laugh at this comment, although he didn't quite manage to pull it off.

Alice elbowed him in the ribs and shot him a stern look. Her steely demeanour dropped a little. 'Well, alright, there have been some very rare occasions where I have been known to engage in gossip. But even if I do, from time to time, I'm certainly not in the habit of sharing it with a journalist like you.'

Margo sighed. 'Oh, come on, Alice. We're all writers here; we all have our own jobs to do. You're not the first person who has taken a personal dislike to me, but you simply must understand that this is not personal, it's business.'

'And Katherine Debenham was one of those, wasn't she?' asked Bertie. 'One of those people who took a personal dislike to you. I was surprised to see you two together at Romano's earlier. We both were,' he added with a nod at Alice.

'Not as surprised as me,' admitted Margo. 'I know she isn't very fond of me; everyone knew that. But I don't take any of that to heart, that's just how it is. There was certainly no reason for me to dislike Katherine as an individual, even though I might have disagreed with her in a professional capacity – how she might interpret the roles she's played. That is my job after all, to critique. I'm more than happy to sit down with anyone if they're willing to speak to me.' She paused a moment. 'It feels terribly strange, talking about things like this, about everything, now that Mr Debenham is no longer with us.'

'Well, no one asked you to. You're free to stop talking at any point,' said Alice, causing a small grimace to pass across Margo's features.

'Look, Katherine invited me to dinner... I think she genuinely wanted to put things behind us. Start afresh. You know it doesn't hurt to be friendly with us journalists,' Margo added, pointedly. 'We want to support artistes; that's our role in all of this at the end of the day, to champion the world of theatre. I think Katherine knew that. That's how it seemed to me. I think that, perhaps, she wanted to move on from the past.'

'Why did she take a dislike to you in the first place? What there a particular reason?' asked Bertie.

'Oh yes!' Before Margo had a chance to begin her own version of events, Alice turned to Bertie with a mischievous grin. 'Don't you remember? She wrote quite the nasty little piece about her a few years ago. How Katherine's marriage was on the cusp of falling apart... It was a real hatchet job, except that it was all nonsense. As we all know, she and Anthony were very much in love. One of the strongest partnerships I know, onstage and off.' She paused, just as Margo had done moments ago, correcting herself. 'Had known, I mean.'

Margo's face fell. 'I wrote that article in good faith. The proof I had ... my sources were impeccable. They—'

'Your sources were wrong,' Alice interrupted. 'We can easily imagine how some young actor spun you a yarn because they bore a grudge. You were used, Margo, I'm sorry to say. You were used.'

'There you go, a playwright inventing their own version of the story – much more interesting that the real thing. Although, yes, in broad strokes, I suppose that's the truth of it,' Margo admitted. 'I was much younger back then, more naïve about things, about life itself. There was plenty I learned from that situation, I can tell you. Now it was regrettable, and almost certainly a reason why Mrs Debenham wasn't one of my biggest fans, but she was the one who wanted to meet up. *She* invited *me*.'

'You arrived at the restaurant a little while after Alice and I did, but from how Katherine Debenham explained it, you must have left the theatre before us?' said Bertie, who had been deep in thought.

'Well, we had arranged to meet at the stage door, right after the matinee.'

'You didn't cancel, with everything that was going on at the theatre?' interjected Bertie.

'No, of course not. Katherine didn't take any of that seriously. She thought it was nonsense. The appointment had been made weeks ago and both of us intended to keep it.'

'I see,' murmured Bertie.

'We met at the theatre and then we set off to Romano's together. It was only a little way along here when she suddenly said it was too chilly and she wanted to go back to collect her coat. We went back to get it and then we set off to Romano's again. That's why we arrived a short while after you, I expect.' She looked between Bertie and Alice as if she was a child making an excuse.

'She asked you to go into the theatre with her?' asked Bertie.

'Well, not really. I just sort of went along with it, I suppose. We were halfway through a conversation about some nonsense... She might have been going on about young people these days, I can't really remember.'

'But you went into her dressing room?' Bertie pushed. 'You saw inside it?'

'No, I didn't go in. I hovered outside. I think her coat must have been hanging on the back of the door; it only took a few moments for her to go in and retrieve it and then we were off again. She didn't even turn the light on, she was in and out so fast.'

'But it was completely empty when you saw it?' said Bertie. 'You got a good view of that?'

'Oh yes. That's what I told the police. It's only a small room. When the door is open there really is nowhere to hide.'

Alice didn't seem convinced. 'You saw right into the dressing room, did you? No one was hidden under any sheets or anything? Behind the curtains?'

'Oh, for goodness' sake. Behind the curtains, Alice?' Margo didn't sound too impressed with Alice's wild theories. 'As improbable as all this seems, don't get it confused with something out of one of your plays. I'm absolutely certain. I got a good enough look at that dressing room; the door was wide open. Even in the gloom it was easy to see it was completely empty.'

Bertie thought carefully. 'She's right. Dennis showed us where he found the body and it was just inside the door. If there was a body in the dressing room, there's absolutely no chance you could have missed it.'

Alice nodded in agreement. 'In that case, he must have gone to her dressing room, for some reason, after you had both left. That's when the murderer made their move. It leaves even less room for opportunity, doesn't it?'

'Who is Dennis?' asked Margo, who had become

more alert. She seemed more concerned about the mention of a new name rather than the mechanics of the case.

'That's none of your business,' responded Alice sharply.

'He's the call boy,' explained Bertie, even though Alice was giving a look in his direction, indicating that she didn't think this was information they should be sharing.

'I wonder if I could speak to him—'

'Absolutely not, Margo,' said Alice, protectively. 'I prohibit it. You can't just hang out on street corners and spend your time harassing people. He's just a boy.'

'That didn't seem to stop you talking to him, did it?' Margo retorted. 'Besides, I'm not "hanging out", I'm waiting. I just want to find out what's going on. The way that policeman was questioning me, it was like he thought I was involved somehow.' She inclined her head slightly, drawing Bertie and Alice's attention across the road. 'I'm also not the only one that's being "hanging out". That chap has been loitering around the stage door for some time now. A fan, do you think? He looks shifty to me.'

Margo was right – across the road was the man Bertie had vaguely recognised in the restaurant. He must have been in his late twenties, but still retained his boyish good looks. However, there was a worried expression on his face. He couldn't seem to decide whether he should keep his hands in his pockets or out of them. The three of them watched him spin on the spot, pause, and turn back again. It seemed as if he couldn't make up his mind as to whether he should stay or if he should go.

'That's not a fan. He's... Well, I'm not quite sure. An actor, I think. How long has he been there?' said Bertie.

Margo took a look at her wristwatch. 'He's been there since I came out, about half an hour ago.'

'Well, you know all the actors, Margo. Isn't that your job?' Alice said, urging her to show off her journalistic skills. 'Who is he?'

'I deal with the well-known actors. Not the ones who play bit parts in the background,' Margo said, cuttingly.

The nervous-looking man reached up and scratched the back of his neck. As he did, his head rose up and he seemed shocked to find that his gaze was returned by three strangers who were staring back at him. He froze, his eyes wide.

Then he ran.

Chapter Eight

8

Bertie stumbled back from the edge of the kerb, knocked back by the rush of wind from a double-decker bus. As it passed along the curve of Aldwych, it blocked him momentarily, preventing him from crossing the road. By the time the vehicle had passed by and his view across the road was clear again, the man that had been hovering outside the theatre was nowhere to be seen.

From his vantage point, Bertie couldn't be sure whether he had hopped onto the back of a passing bus and been whisked away, or if he had simply disappeared round the corner and out of sight.

Finding a gap in the traffic, he quickly set off in pursuit. Alice followed more tentatively behind. When she eventually joined Bertie on the other side, the chase was over before it had begun. There was no way of knowing which direction the man had disappeared in.

Margo made no attempt to cross the road and remained on the other side. All Bertie could do was turn and give a hopeless shrug in response. She leaned against a nearby tree, returning to her previous position with her eyes fixed on the stage door. Bertie supposed she was waiting there in case there was someone else she could accost as they left the theatre.

The two playwrights darted into the stage door entrance, both of them coming to a halt in the small lobby, breathing heavily.

'There was a man outside just now,' Bertie said to the stage door keeper. 'Did you see him?'

The man sat behind a desk that had been built into a square opening in the wall. He lowered his newspaper slowly and deliberately, revealing an impressive Kitchener-sized moustache. He studied Bertie and Alice closely before giving a careful and considered answer. He spoke, slowly. 'Well, seeing as I'm sat inside, at this desk, no, I can't say that I have seen anyone *outside*.'

'No, of course, I was just hoping...' Bertie apologised, catching his breath.

'Perhaps if you'd like to describe him for me, sir, and I'll see if he sounds familiar.' The stage door keeper's suggestion seemed helpful, but delivered in a tone that was laced with sarcasm and didn't sound completely enthusiastic. His newspaper remained held in his hand.

'Late twenties,' Bertie started.

'Dark hair, tall...' Alice added.

'Short,' Bertie corrected.

'Medium height then,' Alice conceded, causing the stage door keeper to sigh.

'Quite good-looking I suppose?'

'Any idea who he is?' asked Alice.

The stage door keeper finally put his newspaper down on the desk – he'd have to finish his crossword later. Instead, he picked up a pipe and began the process of lighting it, speaking between puffs.

'Well, let me see. From that very accurate description...' The comment was accompanied by an unsubtle eye-roll. 'As long as there's been a Gaiety theatre, and as long as there have been Gaiety girls, there's been a steady collection of admirers that congregate outside that stage door. Nothing like it used to be in the olden days, of course. We'd have proper gents in top hats out there, hoping that they might be able to take one of the girls out to dinner. These days, those stage door Johnnies are long gone, and what are we left with? The likes of him, that's what we're bloody left with.'

'And what are the likes of him?' asked Bertie, cautiously interjecting into the grumbling, hoping that he could avoid another rant.

'Having not seen the man, I couldn't say, but I know the type. Fantasists.' His mouth seemed to feel its way around the entire word as he over-enunciated every syllable, gesturing with his pipe for further effect. 'So-called admirers, you might say. Now Mrs Debenham, she was very good about it – not that she had to be. She'd take the time to stop, sign things, talk with them on the way out. Mr Debenham?'

He looked wistfully off, as if he was trying to recall a memory from years ago, rather than something in the last few weeks. 'Well, he did his very best to avoid that sort of attention if he could. We'd often have him leave by the front doors, rather than this way. He'd sit there and wait in the car for her to come round.'

'Do you know the names of any of their regulars or who they might be?'

The stage door keeper thought for a moment, but eventually shook his head. 'Can't say I do. Mrs Debenham might know. They see these same "fans" over and over again; it wouldn't surprise me if she did recognise the description. They often leave letters, gifts, things like that.'

'How regular?' asked Alice.

'Some of them come back night after night... Maybe she shouldn't be so nice to them, encouraging them. That's what keeps them coming back. Your mysterious man was probably just one of them.'

'Could this mystery man have left the threatening note this morning?' said Bertie.

The stage door keeper pointed across the small entrance way to the wall opposite. 'Anyone can leave a note,' he explained. Rows of slim pigeonholes lined the wall, twenty-six in all – one for each letter of the alphabet. 'Could have been any time from late yesterday evening to early this morning. It's down to the actors and theatre staff to collect anything on their way in. Dennis clears out anything that's left every now and then and delivers it to the dressing rooms. If Mr Tay hadn't spotted it, we might not have discovered it for some time.'

'John found it?' asked Bertie, surprised. 'You didn't mention that, Alice.'

'I didn't? Well, perhaps I didn't think it was terribly important at the time. Does it matter who found it?'

'Was the note was addressed to him, as the show's director?'

The stage door keeper shook his head. 'It wasn't addressed to anyone. Someone had simply left it in the "T" slot. He just happened to take it out when he was looking to see if there was anything that had arrived for him and was curious about it. There was no name on it, of course, which was interesting in itself.'

'But we'll never know who put it there, because you didn't see anyone, did you?' Alice sounded a little disappointed in him.

The stage door keeper shook his head and took a few more puffs on his pipe, rapidly filling the small office where he sat with smoke. 'Anything else I can help you with?'

Bertie thought for a moment. 'No. Well actually, about Mr Debenham, did he have many visitors?'

'Yes, he wasn't as popular as his wife in that way, you understand, but perhaps the odd autograph hunter. There was the odd guest he would receive in his dressing room, same as Mrs Debenham. Nothing unusual about that.'

'Can you recall any of them?' asked Bertie.

The stage door keeper sighed again, causing a cloud of grey smoke to appear in front of him. 'Not really. Look, I've told the police all this, I can't keep repeating it all over again, endlessly. I am supposed to maintain some sort of discretion as a stage door keeper, you know.'

'But, considering what's happened?'

'And considering it's us, Hubert...' Alice pushed gently, including his first name, tenderly, for extra effect.

The stage door keeper muttered something incomprehensible under his breath. Clearly, he preferred an easy life and would rather return to his crossword instead of sitting here answering their inane questions. In the hope that the sooner he started, the sooner he might get it over with, he explained in a hushed voice, 'Some of his visitors were friends, although not always. I'd send the call boy up to him and often he would ask me to send them away, although sometimes they insisted.'

'Another reason why, perhaps, he avoided exiting this way?' said Bertie.

'Perhaps,' Hubert repeated back. 'Sometimes he would ask me to pass on a message that he would meet them at his club, rather than here. One or two of them didn't seem that friendly, quite grumpy if you ask me.'

Alice leaned in a little closer. 'What were the grumpy ones here for, I wonder? Chasing down gambling debts? That was always what people said.' She looked between Bertie and the stage door keeper. 'Not that you'd catch me gossiping about that sort of thing,' she added, guiltily.

'Yes, those were always the rumours,' Bertie agreed. 'But old rumours. I thought that was all history now. And you've told the police all of this?' he asked Hubert.

'Of course.' He nodded. 'Not much to go on, is it?'

'I think that one of these visitors could be our killer,' said Alice, tapping the desk with her finger to make the point.

Bertie pondered the idea. 'If it was someone chasing a debt, it would be more likely the other way round, wouldn't it? In that case, Mr Debenham might have been forced to kill to get someone off his back.'

'What if he was forced to defend himself against this person and that's how Mr Debenham got killed, in the struggle? If the tables were turned on him?'

The stage door keeper blew out a cloud of smoke, uninterested in listening to the theories shooting backwards and forwards between the two playwrights. 'Was there anything else?' he said, impatiently.

'Just the movements of people,' said Bertie. 'A quick picture of who went out and when. That would be helpful.'

Alice leaned in. 'We think we know most of it, but it would be good to know for sure. Katherine met Margo Murray here before they went to Romano's.'

'Yes, that's correct.'

'But they arrived there after we did, and we know she came back here to collect her coat.'

'Well, they did return again and when they left Katherine was wearing a coat.' The stage door keeper shrugged, confirming the story.

'She brought Margo in with her,' Bertie added.

'Yes,' said the man, who seemed to be growing a little weary at their barrage of questions.

'Did you hear much of their conversation?' asked Alice.

'Well, I don't know that you could have called it a conversation. More like a monologue, if you ask me. It was very one-sided. I couldn't make out much of what she was saying, but it didn't seem as if Mrs Debenham let that journalist get a word in the whole time.'

'Who else went in and out?' said Bertie.

'If you want a list, we'll be here all day. Pretty much everyone was in and out. The police have taken the signing-in book, so I can't tell you any more than that.'

'Any new faces today?'

The stage door keeper sighed. 'Plenty, I'm afraid. Tonight was supposed to be the last night, so a lot of people pack up their personal things and get them sent on early. There were plenty of new people coming in and out of here, going up and down to the dressing rooms.'

'First nights and last nights.' Bertie smiled. 'The two busiest times for a stage door keeper.'

'That's right,' Hubert agreed. 'It's all flowers and gifts on an opening night, lots of deliveries, lots of new people. The last night, exactly the opposite. Everything starts going back out again. I don't mind of course; there's usually a good tip or two in it for me.'

Bertie turned to Alice. 'And someone who worked in

theatre would have known that, wouldn't they? The perfect cover to slip a note into those pigeonholes without anyone noticing?'

'Of course,' said Alice with a look of realisation. 'If the person who killed Anthony Debenham had some connection to the theatre, they'd know that in between shows on the last matinee day would have been busier and they could have used it as cover to get in and out.'

'Not only that,' said Bertie. 'The advert, all the extra staff that came in as a precaution. That meant the theatre had even more people milling around than usual. With those extra bodies they brought in, it would have meant there was a much larger crowd for someone to disappear in.'

Alice nodded her agreement. 'In all these comings and goings, you didn't notice Anthony Debenham go in and out at any point?'

The stage door keeper shook his head. 'No. I don't think I saw him the rest of the day, not after he'd arrived.'

'Wait, there was one thing,' Bertie said, as a thought had just occurred to him. 'There was a visitor, in between, for Mr Debenham.'

Alice's eyes lit up. 'Oh yes, that's very clever of you to remember that. That's what Dennis said. We saw him before the performance. He went up to Mr Debenham's dressing room and said he had a visitor, but he told Dennis to send him away.'

'That is quite possible,' said the stage door keeper. 'Like I said, there were plenty of comings and goings, so it's hard to keep track of everything. I think Mr Debenham and Mrs Debenham might both have had visitors at the stage door today.'

'Is that something?' asked Alice, looking at Bertie with a hopeful eye.

Bertie returned the look, thinking carefully. 'Hugh told me, in Brighton, just collect the information, as much as you can. Once you've got all the facts, the picture of what went on will finally emerge.'

'Except this time, we don't have Hugh's guidance.'

'No, we don't,' said Bertie.

When he looked back at the stage door keeper to give him his thanks, he had already returned to his crossword.

Chapter Nine

9

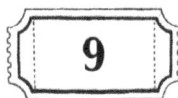

The day had worn relentlessly on and it was getting late. Now, the backstage areas of the theatre had begun to take on a rather gloomy air.

Theatres are living, breathing buildings. They only really come alive when people are passing though their backstage areas and corridors. Like the blood that pumps through our veins, it is the people who bring life to every nook and corner of the building. It makes them tragic, depressing places when they are empty. Then they are merely shells, both devoid of meaning and drained of their essential spirit.

Bertie and Alice, who seemed to be fast approaching the limits of what their investigations could reveal, slowly climbed the stairs to the manager's office. With no one else about it was eerily quiet, except for their footsteps, which could be heard bouncing off the smooth walls.

'I don't like it when it's like this,' Bertie murmured.

'What, when it's all empty like this? Oh no, I love it.'

'Really?'

Alice nodded. 'Yes, it reminds me that a theatre can sometimes be a calm, quiet place. Goodness knows, it doesn't always feel like that when you're in the middle of rehearsals.'

'Well, yes. I'm sure if you could arrange to do plays without actors, directors or any scenery, then rehearsals would be calm, quiet places as well.'

As they reached the top floor, where the office was located, they could hear the voice of Gareth James reverberating along the corridor; he sounded angry. 'You shouldn't have come here.'

The words caused Alice and Bertie to stop in their tracks. They froze automatically where they were, not wanting to make another sound and give themselves away. The office door hadn't quite been closed and even though they were at the far end of the corridor, Gareth's voice could be heard clearly. With a surreptitious glance at each other, they continued to listen carefully.

'You should be grateful,' an unknown male voice replied. 'I didn't have to come here, you know.'

'You shouldn't have. Our business should be conduct-ed elsewhere, not at my place of work. You're not allowed here. We could have done this at some other time, any-where else.'

'To me, it seemed like time was of the essence. As far

as I'm concerned, I don't want to be mixed up with any of this, whatever *this* is. Count yourself lucky that I've come to return this money to you. You can argue I'm not paying you what you're owed, but don't even try it. You know these things would be best left a secret as well as I do. If the police come sniffing round me, I'll know it's you who'll have told them.'

'Fine,' the theatre manager said. 'In that case, let's try not to mention this again.'

There was a moment's pause before the reply came, but when it did you could tell that the man was speaking with a smile, just by the tone of his voice. 'Oh, you'll not mention anything about this business again, I'll make sure of it.'

With that, the door of the office was flung open and a tall figure swept out of it and along the corridor. Bertie and Alice flattened themselves against the wall, letting the man pass between them, but he seemed to pay them no notice.

'What was that about?' Alice mouthed in a half-whisper, once the man had disappeared.

Bertie shrugged in response; he had no idea but he would do his best to find out. He gingerly continued towards the office entrance and Alice followed. Gareth was slumped at his desk, his head resting in his hands. The door had been left open by the rapidly departing visitor and the shuffling movement outside caught his attention. As he lifted his head, he caught sight of Bertie in the opening.

'Oh, Bertie, it's you,' he said, sitting up a little straighter. He sounded a little relieved.

'Yes, and Alice too,' he replied, as Alice tentatively slid into view. Together, they shuffled awkwardly into the room and let the door close behind them.

'I suppose you heard some of that?' asked Gareth. Behind his eyes you could see the mechanics whirring away, trying to calculate how much they might have heard and how much he should reveal.

Alice nodded. 'Some, not all.'

Gareth sighed, holding his hands up. 'I promise you, it's not quite as bad as it sounds.'

'That means it is bad then?' Alice interrupted.

'No,' Gareth insisted. 'It just *looks* bad.'

Gareth indicated the chairs, encouraging them both to sit down. Alice did, however Bertie elected to stay standing.

The theatre manager sighed deeply before beginning. 'You know this theatre is in a bit of a financial hole these days.'

Bertie and Alice nodded; they were well aware of the theatre's financial troubles after a long run of shows that hadn't been terribly well received.

'Because of that, it seemed like a sure thing...' Gareth stopped. 'Sorry, I'm finding it hard to explain, really. Time was you would be able to come across someone in Romano's who would take a wager on pretty much anything. Now, those times have long since passed, but if you know where to look, you can still find someone who is willing to take your bet.'

'And what was it you were betting on?' asked Bertie.

Gareth took a deep breath before answering. 'This show. That it wouldn't see out its full run. It seemed a pretty safe bet, the last five shows haven't managed it. No disrespect to the playwright, of course,' he said, directing the last comment in Alice's direction.

'Disrespect or not, you were wrong – this show did see out its run,' she said.

'Almost,' said Gareth, gravely. 'This evening's show was cancelled, leaving it one performance short. Now, if it *had* completed the run, we'd have been ruined. I'd have lost the money I put up and, quite probably, I would have lost the theatre. In the circumstances, well, it's incorrect to say I've been lucky. But it seems as if we've got off lightly.'

'Quite,' Bertie agreed.

Alice leaned in. 'But he didn't pay up, even though he should have done? No matter what the facts of the matter were, you won your bet.'

'No, he didn't pay up, and under the circumstances... It seems right, don't you think? This way, well, at least we're no worse off than we were at the beginning. Better, in fact. This show of yours, Alice, has done rather well. We might actually turn a profit on this one.'

'How much would you have won, if the show had closed early?' asked Bertie.

Gareth gave a short laugh, almost like a cough, before answering. 'Not a particularly decent amount, I'm afraid. Maybe it would have kept the lights on for a few more months. It wasn't a good bet. It would have lost me more than I would have won, if you see my meaning. Pretty short odds on something like that. Not enough to save us from the financial mess we're in, you understand, but something... Anything. It would have helped. It would have given us enough time, maybe, to help us turn this place around again.'

'I only ask because—'

'Not enough to murder for,' the theatre manager cut Bertie off before he could complete his question. 'I know why you're asking. It doesn't look good, does it?'

'And you've told the police all of this?'

Gareth shuffled in his seat awkwardly; the answer to Bertie's question was obvious. 'No, I haven't.' He held a hand up to stop any further protest from the pair of them. 'I don't think it's relevant.'

Alice's mouth fell open. 'You can't mean that. Of course it's relevant!'

'Look, you two. *I know* I didn't murder Anthony Debenham. Certainly not so that I could win an idiotic wager I should never have made in the first place. I don't see how telling the police about this would help; it would just confuse matters. All that would happen is that suspicion would be cast in my direction and distract them from finding out who really did kill him.' Gareth sighed. 'It is a regrettable and foolish thing that I have done, but now – as you both heard – it has been undone. As far as I'm concerned, that's nearly as good as if it had never happened in the first place. We should let the police get on with the

86

real job at hand here; I think that's for the best, don't you?'

'You don't have any idea who might have killed him?' asked Bertie. 'We know that there were people who visited Anthony. Could one of them have been the same man that we just saw leaving? I wondered if he might have had gambling debts of his own that he needed to settle?'

'No,' said Gareth. 'You think there might have been someone leaning on him for the money, but perhaps they leaned a little too hard and it went wrong? Is that what you mean?'

Bertie nodded.

'As far as I knew, Anthony's gambling days were behind him. Yes, he used to get in all sorts of trouble years back, but I thought that had all been smoothed over now.'

'Unless he's fallen back into old habits,' Alice interjected. 'These things do happen.'

'Those gambling days...' Bertie looked from Gareth back to Alice. 'That would all have been around the time of Margo's article? When was that? Five or six years ago?'

Gareth nodded. 'Yes, that's right, around then.'

'She was wide of the mark in regard to the strength of their relationship,' said Alice, thinking out loud, 'but maybe there was a division in their relationship, driven apart by Anthony's gambling. Could that be what was really going on and she just read the whisperings incorrectly?'

'That sounds plausible,' agreed Bertie. 'But I don't know if that gets us any closer to a real motive, or even a suspect. In the end they managed to smooth it over, together – Katherine in the driving seat, I imagine. Since then, their relationship has been stronger than ever.'

'Unless there was something from the past,' Gareth said. 'Some debt not quite cleared, some score to be settled. Something they overlooked.'

Bertie looked at him with a serious expression on his face. 'Once you get in with these people, Gareth, it's a slippery slope.'

'Yes, I'm afraid my recent experience means that's something I know too well. Shall we say: lesson learned, on my part anyway. I won't be doing anything like that again any time soon.'

'And the theatre, it will be alright?' asked Alice.

'If you write me another show as good as this one.' Gareth chuckled, before returning to a serious voice. 'One more good show, that's all we need, then we're back in the black. Fortunes do turn around in this business, you just need a bit of luck. If I'd known that placing an advert like that would have drawn a sell-out crowd, I would have done it weeks ago.'

'But you have no idea who did place it?' said Alice, leaning in.

'No idea.' Gareth rose from his chair. 'Come on, it's late. We better think about locking up this place for the night.'

Bertie and Alice automatically stood up, following his lead.

'And this little business of the wager,' he said,

conspiratorially. 'We can keep that between us.'

Bertie shook his head as he opened the office door to let them out. 'I can't make that promise I'm afraid, Gareth.'

'But it's not relevant, Bertie, I can promise you that. It's not.'

'But what if it *does* become relevant?' Bertie left the question hanging in the air. 'I'm afraid that in that case, we wouldn't be prepared to keep it a secret. We couldn't.'

Alice had already begun to head out through the door but turned to agree with Bertie. 'Quite right too. I'm sorry Gareth, I think he's right on this one. If you have any sense, you'll tell the police first thing tomorrow so this is all out in the open. If you really have nothing to hide, you have nothing to be afraid of.'

'But I don't have anything to hide.' Gareth was almost pleading now. 'It would just complicate matters, and as you can quite clearly see, I didn't benefit from Anthony's death.'

'No, you didn't benefit from Anthony's death,' said Bertie, deep in thought.

Gareth nodded. 'Exactly.'

Bertie followed Alice out into the corridor but turned back to Gareth with one last thought. 'You could have done, in fact you should have done. There was still money to be gained from the wager if the show didn't finish its run. By your own admission, it wouldn't have been a significant amount. Enough to keep things going for a short while, but not enough to secure the long-term future of this theatre. Just to keep the lights on for another month or two.'

'Quite, Bertie,' said Gareth. 'It certainly wouldn't have been an amount that was worth killing for.'

Bertie closed the door behind him. When it had clicked shut, Alice turned to him.

'So, off or on the suspects list then?'

He nodded gently. 'On, I'd say. Definitely on.'

'I know it would have only been a small amount, but that's still worth winning, isn't it?' asked Alice.

'It wasn't about winning that bet though, was it? Where did he get the money to place it? From this show's takings? That was a big risk. It was a bet he couldn't afford to lose. He said, just now, in his own words, that there was far more to be lost than gained. If things had gone the other way and this show had reached the end of its run, he would have lost everything. He would have been ruined; almost certainly he would have lost this theatre. I don't know...'

Bertie looked at the closed office door, a new theory slowly forming in his mind.

Alice leaned forward. 'What are you thinking?'

'Preventing that from happening certainly would have been worth killing for.'

Chapter Ten

10

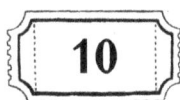

Descending the stairs in silence, Alice and Bertie made their way down to the stage door. As they turned the final corner, a familiar figure caused Bertie to jump. Sam had been leaning casually against the wall, one foot raised and pressed against it. He was similarly startled by the appearance of the two playwrights and stood up straight, stubbing the cigarette he had been smoking out in a slim metal ashtray that was screwed to the wall, next to the pigeonholes. He straightened his flat cap.

'Someone mentioned that you might still be here,' the flyman said, perhaps with a little too much eagerness in his voice. He quickly tried to cover it by forcing a serious expression, but he couldn't quite stop his smile from breaking back through.

'Hello, Sam,' said Alice. 'I think perhaps I'll leave you

two to it. Expect me to call tomorrow morning, Bertie. Let's see if we can make a plan about what we might do next?' With a knowing look at Bertie, and after a farewell nod, Alice swept out through the exit.

Bertie, who was stuck somewhere between feeling abandoned and set up, smiled awkwardly.

Sam returned a similar grin. 'I don't suppose...' he started. 'Look. Maybe you would like to...' He sighed. 'I don't know, I seem to be doing this all wrong. Did you want to go somewhere?'

'Somewhere?'

'You know, for a drink?' Sam scratched the stubble on his chin before adding, 'With me?'

Bertie smiled 'Do you know a place?'

Sam nodded. 'Yeah, there's this club in Endell Street, not far from here.'

'Yeah... I mean, yes,' said Bertie, stumbling over his words. This was all very sudden and unexpected. He wondered what snippets of information Alice had been slipping to Sam during the course of the rehearsals, while she had been hidden away on the fly floor. He didn't appreciate her rather unsubtle attempt at matchmaking.

'Great. That's great.' Sam broke into a wide smile, which was infectious, causing Bertie to laugh. Bertie led the way out, throwing a final farewell glance at the stage door keeper, who seemed to be doing a rather good job of ignoring the two of them, who were now giggling like schoolboys.

As the two of them emerged from out of the stage

door, the sunlight had very nearly faded and the sky had turned a deep dark blue. It was dim enough that the street-lamps had already been lit.

A glossy black car was parked on the street with a man leaning against it, his attention drawn by the loud noise of the stage door banging open and the two laughing figures emerging from it. They were both quickly silenced as they saw the man, who stood up straighter and took a few steps forward into the warm pool of light being cast downwards by the streetlamp.

It was Hugh.

He had opened his mouth, ready to speak, but closed it again once he realised Bertie was not by himself. The gap left between them, where no one said anything, was long enough to be awkward. Bertie couldn't quite inter-pret Hugh's expression. It was somewhere in between embarrassment and disappointment.

Hugh was the first person who spoke. 'Hello, Bertie.'

Bertie wasn't quite sure how to respond, so he raised a hand, as if to say *one moment*, and turned to speak quietly to Sam.

As he turned, Bertie could already see Sam carefully analysing the two of them, his eyes narrowed and sliding between the two of them. 'I see,' Sam said, before Bertie could say anything, sounding a little despondent.

'You do?' asked Bertie.

'Two people with a history and something to get off their chests... I know that look all too well.'

'Another time, perhaps?' Bertie said, politely,

although he felt it was little consolation.

'I guess I'll see you around.' Sam turned, wandering off with his shoulders hunched. As he departed, he turned his body so he was walking backwards, getting one last look at the pair of them. His eyes drifted from Bertie to Hugh as he tried to work out what could possibly be going on between a playwright and a police detective. He attempted one last wave goodbye, although didn't quite manage it as he spun on his heels, rounded the corner and disappeared from view.

Hugh shifted his weight from one foot to the other, awkwardly. 'I didn't mean to...' he started, reading the situation correctly. 'I'm sorry.'

'It's alright.' Bertie sighed, forcing a smile to his face.

'I heard you were still around and I'm actually heading up your way,' Hugh said, in a brighter tone. 'Fancy a lift?'

'Really?'

Hugh opened the door, indicating that Bertie should get in. 'Really.'

Bertie climbed into the back of the vehicle, admiring its large, squashy, red leather seats. It was easy to slide over and make space for Hugh to join him. Once they were both inside, Hugh rapped twice on the glass window that separated them from the police driver, who set off immediately.

It's strange how everything always looks unfamiliar in the dark. The streets and buildings that Bertie knew well somehow became unrecognisable once the sun had set and a different kind of light was cast over them.

The glow from the passing streetlamps illuminated Hugh's face in brief flashes. The interior of the car was too dark to be able to read his expression, even though he was sitting close by.

They rounded the corner at the British Museum and were well on their way to Regent's Park before Bertie made an attempt to strike up conversation. 'I did...' he started. 'I tried to get in touch with you. My swimming technique has improved since I've been practising. Now the weather's a bit warmer, I did wonder if you ever wanted to join me? An excuse for a chance to meet up occasionally. I didn't want it to be another ten years before we spoke again.'

Hugh sighed. 'I'm afraid I've rather given up on swimming,' he said, avoiding Bertie's gaze.

'Really?'

He nodded. 'Yes. I've got back into boxing, recently.'

'Oh, I see,' said Bertie, unable to hide a knowing smile. 'I suppose that's something that's more appropriate for someone in your position?'

'That's not why—'

'Something more manly,' Bertie interrupted, a little petulantly. He regretted it almost instantly, but the months of silence had built up a slight resentment in him that he was struggling to contain.

Hugh twisted his body in his seat to face Bertie. 'That's not it at all.' He froze, unsure what to say next. Giving a glance at the driver and then back to Bertie, he decided to face the front and be silent again.

Bertie reached out delicately in the gloom, to get a better look at the cut above Hugh's eye. 'I suppose that explains this then...'

Hugh gently guided the enquiring hand away, moving it back to Bertie's side before it could reach his face. He let his own hand hover there for a moment, encouraging Bertie to keep his hands in place.

'I'm no expert, but I thought the idea of boxing was *not* to get hit by your opponent?' said Bertie.

'Well, yes, that's generally what you're aiming for. I'm afraid I'm not as sharp as I used to be. Although, with more practice, I'm getting better all the time.'

'I don't know why you didn't mention it. I could have, I don't know... I could have come to support you. It looks like you could do with the help.'

Hugh let out a sharp breath of amusement, as if the last place he would expect to find Bertie was at a boxing hall.

'What?' asked Bertie. He didn't seem to think the idea was all that ridiculous.

'Sorry. I didn't mean to find it funny. It's just...' Hugh stopped talking, realising that he was still holding Bertie's hand in place. He relinquished his grip gently, returning his hand to his own lap. 'It's not exactly your scene, is it?'

Bertie let his mind drift back to Sam and the type of place where they might have ended up in Endell Street. Predominately male, certainly things would start to get a little loud and often quite raucous once the drinks started flowing. Was that really a world away from the crowd you'd find at a boxing match? Hugh hadn't been wrong though: a boxing hall wouldn't have been on the list of places he regularly attended. Bertie couldn't imagine himself attending that kind of establishment, just as he couldn't imagine Hugh appearing in some of the venues he frequented. The thought seemed to lodge itself in his mind, awkwardly.

'Where are we going?' asked Bertie.

'Lawn Road, right around the corner from you. I need to talk to a Mr Danny Owen who currently resides there.'

'Danny Owen!' exclaimed Bertie in sudden realisation, causing Hugh to turn to him in surprise. 'Danny-bloody-Owen. I knew I recognised that face outside the theatre today, at the stage door. He ran away when I tried to chase him.'

Hugh didn't say anything and merely watched with amusement. He gave a nod of the head, indicating to Bertie that he should continue.

'He was at Romano's earlier today too; I saw him there when I was with Alice. I couldn't quite put a name to the face. But of course, Danny Owen... He's an actor, or at least he was at some point. I'm not sure what he gets up to now.'

Hugh smiled. 'Yes, some other people mentioned that they had seen him when we talked to them. The fact that he was there today might well have something to do with why we're on our way to talk to him.'

'*We're*, Hugh?'

'It's not escaped my notice that you've been doing some investigating yourself. Perhaps we should go and see Mr Owen together. Then afterwards, maybe we could talk a while and compare our notes.'

'I see. The detective finally admits that he needs some of my expert help?' Bertie said jokingly.

Hugh smiled. 'Well, that's not what I said at all.'

'How on earth did you connect Danny to the murder?' Bertie asked.

'We haven't, yet,' admitted Hugh, 'but as you said, he was at the theatre and Romano's too. That certainly makes him a person that's of interest to us.'

'Yes, but a thousand other people were at the theatre today. What makes you think he had anything to do with it?'

'We know he tried to get backstage but was turned away, so we want to know why.'

'Perhaps *he* was Anthony's visitor?' said Bertie, who was deep in thought. Unlike Hugh, who he imagined had been writing everything down in his notebook precisely, Bertie hadn't thought to do that and was relying on his memory.

'Visitor?' Hugh asked.

'Yes, Alice and I overheard it before the show. Dennis, he's the call boy, came up to Mr Debenham's dressing room and he said there was a visitor at the stage door, but Anthony asked for him to be sent away.'

'Well, that's useful.' Hugh nodded, taking in the new information. 'We couldn't quite unpick who was visiting who earlier on.'

'The stage door keeper seemed to think they both received visitors at the theatre today, although that's not exactly unusual for someone in their position. I'm sure they often had guests.'

'Yes, it seems they were both quite popular.'

'Well, they are.' Bertie quickly corrected himself. 'Were. Katherine had worked more than Anthony in recent years, but I think both of them would have relished being in a play that's had such a successful run.'

'And greeting guests at the theatre, that would allow them to show off a little?'

'Why not? Although, I don't know why someone like Danny Owen would be visiting him.'

'Not of their social standing, you mean?'

'I wouldn't want to be unkind, Hugh, but he's not in the same league as Anthony or Katherine. Of course, this is a tiny industry. There's no reason why he shouldn't have met them and become acquainted over the years. I wonder what he could have been visiting Anthony about.'

'We'll find out in a few minutes,' said Hugh, taking a look out of the car window. 'What happened when he came to visit? You said you heard Mr Debenham turning him away?'

Bertie nodded. 'Anthony said "not now" and told the call boy to send him on his way.'

'When we spoke to the stage door keeper he said he couldn't remember who Mr Owen was there to see or why, and he didn't seem to notice who left that damned note either.'

'Hmm, I didn't think too much of his observational skills,' said Bertie. 'And what do your observational skills tell you about me? I take it that they've led you to the conclusion that I couldn't possibly be involved in this murder.'

'I'm afraid, Bertie, that I can't quite say that for sure,' Hugh said, with the barest hint of a smile. 'Let's just say that I've decided to trust you.'

Chapter Eleven

11

The police car slowed and pulled up alongside a sleek white building as Hugh and Bertie's conversation came to a close. Its smooth, bright walls were gleaming and pristine. Even in the dark, they seemed to be glowing in the moonlight.

Together, they got out of the car and crossed the pavement. As they stepped onto the forecourt, Bertie was surprised to find what felt like loose gravel under their feet. Now the crisp white walls made some more sense: they were recently painted and the building was still in the final stages of its construction. It seemed as if the exterior had been finished but the area in front of the building was awaiting its final top layer of macadam or cement.

As they approached, his gaze drifted up to the building that rose above them. It had been built in the modern style with open walkways that stretched along the front of it. The whole thing seemed to defy gravity; the long balconies looked like they were floating, unsupported in mid-air.

At the end of the building a staircase curved and zig-zagged its way up the outside. His eyes followed it up to the full height of the building – four or five floors. Scanning the facade, it looked like only one of the flats had its lights on. On the first floor, the dim glow, visible around the edges of the closed curtains, stood out against the dark of the rest of the building. The rest of the place appeared to be empty. After they climbed up and made their way along the walkway, Hugh rapped sharply on the door and after a few moments the inquisitive head of Danny Owen appeared round it. He held the door only slightly ajar, wary of any visitors arriving at this time of night.

He looked enquiringly at Hugh. 'Yes?'

'Mr Owen, I am Detective Chief Inspector Hugh Chapman. I was wondering if we could come in and have a few words? This is—'

'It's Bertie-bleeding-Carroll!' Danny exclaimed, with an enthusiastic grin. 'Come in, come in.' He threw the door wide open, inviting them in. As he did so, he revealed the rest of his figure. He looked rather bedraggled with his shirt half untucked, a glass in his hand, and appearing a little worse for wear. Bertie suspected that the half-empty glass wasn't his first of the night.

'Do you two know each other?' asked Hugh, the comment laced with a hint of humour, as he stepped into the tiny studio flat.

'I'd hardly say that,' Bertie replied, under his breath.

Danny responded much more enthusiastically. 'Don't be silly, of course we do! That said, it was only once and quite a few years ago.'

Hugh raised his eyebrows. 'Is that right?'

'It would have been, what... Eight, nine years ago?'

'Nothing more recently than that? Might you have bumped into each other earlier today?' Hugh said, the hint of amusement growing in his voice.

Danny chose to ignore the question. 'Let me get you a drink? I'm afraid I've not got much in the way of choice.' He waved his arm vaguely in the direction of a decanter on the side. Bertie caught Hugh's expression; he was clearly thinking the same as him. Judging by Danny's current, inebriated state, they both suspected that it would have contained far more liquid at the start of the evening.

'Sit down, sit down,' Danny encouraged. The influence of alcohol made his hand movements a little more over the top than necessary. Bertie and Hugh sat in the only two chairs that had been placed in the room. Danny added a generous slosh of the amber liquid from the decanter to his glass. He held the decanter up, waving it towards Bertie and Hugh in a final offer at joining him for a drink. They declined and he simply shrugged his shoulders before returned it to the side with a thud. Since there were no other seats available in the room, he perched on the edge of the bed across from them.

Danny looked off into the distance as he attempted to

recall a memory. 'It was when I was still training, right, Bertie? The Central School at the Albert Hall. We were doing an early version of one of your plays, trying it on for size or something like that. Of course, it was well before you became the huge success you are now.'

'Yes, that's it,' Bertie recalled. 'I knew there was a reason I recognised you, but I couldn't remember where it was from.'

Danny shifted uncomfortably on the bed, scratching the back of his neck with his free hand. 'Yes, well... Not exactly had the best of luck with work since leaving and all that. But these things happen. Such is the life of an actor.'

Hugh pointed at the glass in Danny's hand. 'How much have you had to drink tonight?'

'Not enough, I'd say,' Danny joked.

'It's just interesting, isn't it? To be drinking this much on a day when someone has been murdered, at a theatre that you visited earlier on that same day?'

'In that case, I'd like to have invited you here yesterday evening and probably the day before that. I think you'd find that this is very much a character trait of mine. I'm an out-of-work actor, with very few job prospects.' He held the glass up, peering at Hugh through it. 'Now, this might be an unwise vice but, all too often, it is a necessary one.'

Danny paused a moment, delicately lowering the glass to get a clearer look at the detective, finally registering the words he had spoken. 'Murder, did you say?'

Hugh nodded. 'Yes, Anthony Debenham was found, murdered, earlier today at the theatre he was performing at.'

'God,' said Danny, looking a little paler. 'Well, I'm sorry to hear that.'

'Tell me, Mr Owen, how does an out-of-work actor afford to live in a place like this?'

Danny gave a wry chuckle. 'Mr Inspector... I might not be getting that much work as an actor, but I do enough to get by.'

'What kind of things?' asked Bertie.

'This and that. I thought for a while I might even try my hand at your sort of thing.'

Bertie looked surprised. 'Playwriting?'

'Writing, certainly. A novel perhaps. I thought, why not give it a go?' Danny nodded his head, drawing attention towards a stack of blank paper that was sitting on the side, still waiting to be typed on.

'Well, they do say that getting started is the hardest part,' Bertie said encouragingly.

'You've been living here how long?' asked Hugh.

'Only a few weeks. You've seen outside, it's not quite finished yet, but I've got a friend... They were very kindly able to pull a few strings and get me in here before the official opening.' He looked around the room. 'It's all based around some new concept: minimal living, that's what they call it. That's how they designed everything. Tiny kitchen, tiny bathroom, the bare minimum of everything required for one to live and not a crumb more.'

Hugh nodded. 'And before this, where were you living?'

Danny stared down at the liquid in his glass as he swirled it around. 'Here and there.' He looked up at Hugh and noticed he didn't quite seem satisfied with the answer. 'I stay with friends. People who are willing to help a chap out. Spare rooms, sofas, that sort of thing.'

'When I saw you at Romano's earlier today, you were dining alone,' said Bertie. 'None of these friends of yours wanted to join you?'

Danny tilted his head. 'Now then, Bertie. There's no need to be unkind about it.'

'I promise you, I wasn't trying to be. I was merely making an observation: there was no one with you.'

'I was sitting by myself, yes.' Danny placed his glass, which had quickly been drained, on the side table next to the bed. 'Although you're never really alone at Romano's, are you? It's the place to meet people, the place to be seen. Plenty of theatrical deals have been done in that place – long may that continue. Sometimes you just need to be in the right place at the right time to pick up a bit of work. I suppose you might say that I was just increasing my odds.'

'And did you?' asked Hugh. 'Meet anyone, I mean?'

Danny exhaled and chuckled. 'No. Like I said, even though I manage to survive, things haven't exactly gone my way in terms of the acting business lately.'

Hugh leaned forward a little. 'You were also at the Gaiety, earlier in the day. What were you doing there?'

'I was, was I?' Danny's eyes narrowed, but he didn't elaborate any further.

'Yes, at the stage door, trying to get in and see Mr Debenham,' said Bertie.

'Can you tell me what your reason for being there was?' Hugh asked.

'Seeing Mr Debenham? Well, it looks like you already know all about it, don't you?' Danny paused and thought for a moment. 'There wasn't a reason. I mean, I wasn't in town to meet anyone specifically, it just so happened that I was passing by. Why shouldn't I pop and see Anthony Debenham?'

Bertie watched on closely as Hugh asked his questions.

'You just happened to be passing by?'

Danny smiled. 'If you move in theatrical circles and you're wandering through the West End, you're likely to bump into all manner of people. I thought, of all people, why not bump into Anthony? You never know, it might lead to something.'

'So, you're friendly with the Debenhams?' asked Hugh.

'I wouldn't say I'm particularly close with Mr Debenham. We've met socially a few times. Like I said, we all move in the same circles in this business, don't we?'

'And Mrs Debenham?'

'The same.'

'Friendly?' clarified Hugh.

'Why wouldn't I be?' Danny smiled.

'You didn't get a chance to see Mr Debenham in the end, did you?' asked Bertie.

Danny narrowed his eyes a little, inspecting Bertie closely before he answered, 'No.'

'He didn't want to see you; he turned you away?'

'Well, you certainly seem to know about everything. I don't know why you need me,' Danny answered, with a smile. 'Yes, you're right. I didn't get to see him.'

'And you really had no specific reason you wanted to see him? Nothing you particularly wanted to talk about with him?'

'I told you, Bertie, there was no reason. I was just passing by. Why not pop by and give him my best wishes on having had a long and successful run? These things sometimes lead to more. A job, a role, a part. Maybe he needed a picture hanging, I don't know. Work. That's what I suppose I wanted. Work.'

'And during the matinee?' Hugh asked. 'Where did you go after you were turned away from the theatre?'

'Here and there.'

'Mr Owen, I urge you to push yourself and try to think of something more specific,' said Hugh, unimpressed with his answer.

'Out and about.' Danny smiled; it would have been enchanting if he wasn't being so annoying.

'You didn't stay to watch the performance?'

'I would if I could have done. No chance of getting a ticket, was there?' Danny shrugged. 'The whole thing was completely sold out.'

'You didn't meet anyone, bump into someone else who might have recognised you? Someone who can confirm your whereabouts?'

'Like I said, I was just around. Haven't you ever taken a slow aimless walk yourself, Inspector? Sometimes it's just what's needed to think things through.'

Sensing he wouldn't get an answer, Hugh moved on. 'Then perhaps you can tell me where you were after the matinee performance had ended?'

While Hugh asked his question, Danny had retrieved a cigarette from a luxurious-looking silver case that he kept on the side table. He let it hang loosely in his mouth, unlit, while he thought. 'I reckon that by the time the curtain would have fallen on the matinee, I was already in Romano's. When I arrived there, it hadn't got busy so people were probably still in their shows.'

'And can anyone confirm that?'

Danny took his time, striking a match and bringing it up to the end of his cigarette. Once it was lit, his attention moved back to the other side of the room. 'Why don't you ask a waiter?' he asked dryly, but then gave a smile though a cloud of smoke. 'Or Bertie? I think you can vouch for me?'

Bertie sighed. 'He's right, Hugh. It does all fit together. I know he was already there when Alice and I arrived. That was before Katherine and Margo arrived, and we know the dressing room was still empty at that point. There's no way he could have slipped back to the theatre and murdered Anthony Debenham in that time.'

'Still, Mr Owen, I would like you to attend Scotland Yard tomorrow so we can have your fingerprints taken.' Hugh retrieved a card from his inside jacket pocket and handed to him.

With a smile on his face, Danny put on a fake Cockney accent – Bertie thought it was pretty terrible. 'You think I was the one what done it, do ya?' He laughed gently, returning to his normal voice again, then spoke softly. 'Oh no, I think I can say for certain it definitely wasn't me.'

Chapter Twelve

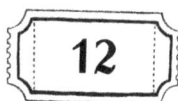

12

After being crammed in that stuffy room, the night air outside seemed clean and fresh. Bertie took a deep breath, turned, and smiled at Hugh. 'I assume you're going to be a gentleman and walk me home?'

'Yes,' Hugh replied, looking down at the empty space where the police car which had dropped them off had been. 'Perhaps I didn't quite think things through when I sent the car away. I promised you a lift home, but I guess a walk home will have to do instead.'

'It's not far,' said Bertie.

'I know.'

At this time of night, the streets were silent and empty. There was no traffic, no people. Even the trees that lined the streets stood still, with no wind to rustle them. Not for the first time, when Bertie found himself alone with Hugh, it felt like there was no one else in the world.

'I'm glad we're talking again,' said Bertie. He said it with a smile, but it was clear that there was a marked pointedness to the comment.

Hugh looked to the sky, in an expression of mock exasperation. 'At the theatre, someone had just been murdered. I was working.'

'And now?'

'Well, now...' Hugh looked at his watch and smiled, 'I'm off duty. Like I said, this isn't like Brighton. Things are different this time. I wasn't with you when the murder took place; I was last time. For all I know, you could still be the murderer.'

'I thought you said that you'd decided to trust me. You still haven't ruled me out completely then?' asked Bertie.

Hugh chuckled. 'Not at the moment. But I suppose the reasons for getting you involved are the same as last time. As my own personal expert in the theatre, you could be useful.'

'So that's the only reason? You wanted to bring me to see Danny Owen, just in case I could provide some further insight?'

'Partly, but also, we really were going your direction. I thought, why not give you a ride?'

'Well, now I've apparently earned back your trust, perhaps we can share what we know with each other.'

Hugh smiled. 'Perhaps.'

Bertie started first. 'Well, what I know is that after the

show, Katherine and Margo returned to her dressing room, which Margo was able to confirm was empty. That narrows down the time of the murder. Then they arrived at Romano's and were in sight of Alice and me the entire time. Now, at some point between them leaving the theatre and you showing up, Anthony Debenham was murdered in Katherine's dressing room, discovered by Dennis. So, by my reckoning, that eliminates all five of us: me, Alice, Margo, Katherine and Danny. That proves I'm innocent – the others, too. Who else is left? John Tay and Gareth James – the director and the manager?'

Hugh looked impressed. 'Well, well... You have been busy, haven't you?'

'If there's more to Danny Owen, I'm not quite sure how it fits in. It's an odd coincidence, him coming to visit, being turned away, and Mr Debenham ending up murdered.'

'About Danny Owen...' Hugh started, tentatively. 'Some people might say that he is a good-looking man.'

'Some people?'

'I just wonder how someone like that, who hasn't had a steady job since graduating from drama school, might be making ends meet? Living in a fancy new building, drinking from a fancy crystal decanter and smoking cigarettes—'

'From an expensive-looking cigarette case,' said Bertie, completing Hugh's train of thought. 'Why didn't you ask him?'

Hugh sighed. 'There didn't seem much point; he'd

have just given me some lie or other.'

'You didn't believe a lot of what he was saying, did you?'

'Not much of it, I'm afraid. I just wondered if there was anything more between him and Mr Debenham.'

'What? As some kind of paramour, you mean?' Bertie almost laughed at the idea of it. 'No, I don't think that's the case.'

'Just a thought.'

'And the fingerprints?' Bertie asked. 'Why do you want his fingerprints? Do you really think he could have done it?'

Hugh sighed. 'I think he's as likely as anyone else at this stage. So far, we haven't found a match for the marks left on that letter opener.'

'You haven't taken mine,' said Bertie.

'No, it's not come to that yet, but maybe we will have to,' Hugh said in a voice that Bertie interpreted as a joke, but easily might not have been.

'I suppose, in the course of your questioning, you've discovered Mr Debenham's shady past. His gambling.'

Hugh nodded. 'And now we come across someone who appears to have a little more money than they should have... It's an intriguing idea. Could it be that Mr Owen has been having more luck and making a living that way? Were the two related? Was he trying to meet up with Mr Debenham to claim his winnings from him?'

'We – by which I mean those of us in the theatre trade – had thought those days were long behind him.'

'Perhaps the past isn't as far behind him as you originally thought.'

Bertie let out a small laugh. 'It's funny, for years we thought the Debenhams were the perfect couple. Charming, loyal, dedicated to each other, but maybe there was a hidden part to them and we had no idea.'

'I think you will find there are plenty of couples out there that have secrets. Plenty of people out there who have a side to their lives that they don't want to share. Perhaps they are not ready or willing to.' Hugh paused. 'Perhaps a side of their life they *can't* share.'

Bertie glanced over at Hugh, who seemed to be concentrating on the pavement ahead of him. 'Some people and their jobs. Actors, say. They've got a public persona to protect. In this case, it makes sense that they would want to keep things under wraps. Protect their marriage as well as their work.'

'You tell me, Bertie. The theatrical profession isn't always free of scandal. Would something like this really make much of a difference?'

'It might. Especially as the two of them have managed to cultivate such a squeaky-clean image over the years. It might be why their agent was pushing for them to be in the play together, a show of unity...'

'Is that right?' asked Hugh.

'Oh, yes. That's what Alice told me, that they came as a pair or not at all. Anthony hadn't had much work in recent years—'

'And this could have been her attempt to get him back

on the straight and narrow?' Hugh interrupted.

'Getting him back on the stage again, at least. Perhaps it might have encouraged him not to return to an old vice before it got too serious.'

'You and Alice?' asked Hugh, surprising Bertie with the conversational change in direction. 'Are you just friends, or...?' He left the question hanging in mid-air.

Bertie laughed so loudly it echoed down the road. 'Hugh, you know I'm not—' Seeing the look on Hugh's face caused Bertie to stop talking.

'I just thought, maybe, I don't know. She seems like a good friend.'

Bertie smiled. 'She *is* a good friend. Actually, she's a very good enemy. We're supposed to be bitter rivals; our plays are always put in competition with each other. Some days, I admit, it feels a little bit more like that than others, especially when we have shows that are opening at the same time.' He became more serious. 'Look, I know I've never exactly said anything to you.'

Hugh breathed out. 'You never had to.'

Bertie shrugged, not knowing what to say.

Hugh laughed. 'Bertie, over all those years and all the cigarette cards I used to let you keep when we were at school. Boxers, association football. It wasn't like you took an interest in the sport...'

Clearly Bertie had never been quite as subtle as he had thought. As he looked up, he caught Hugh's eye, causing them both to laugh out loud. 'You were always a brilliant detective, Hugh.'

'I suppose I knew that there was something different about you. I don't even know what the word is. I know the letter of the law, and what they call it there is "gross indecency". But that doesn't seem to bear any relation to the man standing in front of me today.'

'No. It doesn't.'

Hugh swallowed, not quite able to meet Bertie's eyes. 'And your friend, from the stage door, earlier tonight. Is he just a friend, too?'

Bertie felt like laughing again but managed to contain himself. 'I'm getting quite the grilling, aren't I?' All the same, the situation felt quite serious. 'He's... Well, I'm not sure he's anything. We only met for the first time today.'

'I won't ask where you were going, in case I'm obliged to report it.' Hugh stopped walking, turned to Bertie and put a hand on his shoulder, gripping it tightly. 'Promise me. You will be careful, won't you, Bertie?'

'Of course,' Bertie said, dismissively, looking down at the ground.

'Promise me,' Hugh repeated, giving Bertie a gentle but firm shake, which encouraged him to look up into Hugh's pleading eyes.

'I promise.'

'Good,' said Hugh. He held Bertie's gaze a little longer, before releasing his grip. For a moment, his hand hovered next to Bertie's jaw. There was no contact, but Bertie could feel it next to him. It almost felt like Hugh wanted to let his hand brush against Bertie's cheek in an act of comfort.

It was so brief, and Hugh had already turned to continue along the road, that Bertie couldn't be sure that anything had happened at all. Hugh strode quickly ahead and Bertie had to do a little jog to catch him up.

'Murderers return to the scene of the crime, don't they?' Bertie said, returning the subject back to the murder. 'It just reminds me of Danny Owen and that we saw him hovering around the stage door. When we approached him, he ran. That's not the behaviour of an innocent man, is it?'

'That's true, but before you get carried away with that theory, think it through. I know the stage door keeper isn't the most observant man in the world, but he would have known Mr Owen. After all, he would have been the one to turn him away when Mr Debenham didn't want to see him. He would have recognised him if he had tried to get into the building again, later. Other actors would have recognised him as well – you did.'

Bertie felt a little disheartened but nodded in agreement. Hugh did seem to be talking sense.

'The other thing that I keep coming back to is that all this happened in Mrs Debenham's dressing room,' said Hugh. 'If it was someone out to get Mr Debenham, surely they would have been more likely to attack him in his own dressing room, otherwise how would they know where to find him?'

Bertie sighed. 'This is much harder than last time, Hugh, and that wasn't easy.'

'Well, last time we actually saw the murder being

committed. That helped.' Hugh smiled. 'You can have as many theories or ideas as you want, but there will only be one that fits all the facts. All the details have to line up. That's why we've got detailed notes of everything in her dressing room, Mr Debenham's too. In all the information we've gathered, we don't know what's important yet, but there will only be one solution that will make sense of it all. I don't think we're there yet.'

As Hugh finished, they came to a stop outside the gate to Bertie's building.

'And what was in her dressing room?' asked Bertie.

'Well, not much, to be honest. Most personal belongings were packed up, ready to be collected at the end of the show tonight. There were all the costumes from the show, makeup, two glasses and a bottle of champagne.'

'That sounds about right. I know Mr Debenham went down to join her after the show.'

'And for that part of the mystery, the evidence fits the story.'

'Do you want to...' Bertie tailed off, pointing in the direction of the building. 'Do you want to come up for a bit? Keep talking through the case?'

Hugh shook his head. 'I'll walk you to the door.'

They walked along the short path that curved towards the front door. In the dim glow of the lamp that lit the entrance, Bertie inserted his door keys and then stopped. 'Brighton,' he said. 'I just wanted to ask...'

'Yes,' Hugh encouraged him to continue.

'In the end, we got distracted by the murder and

everything, so I never got a chance to ask. I haven't been able to ask since then either, because this is the first time we've been able to talk. Why did you call me out of the blue? Why did you want to meet up again after all these years?'

Hugh looked serious for a moment. 'Bertie.' He smiled. 'You're my oldest friend. I hadn't seen you in the best part of a decade. I thought it was time to have a reunion.'

'I thought maybe—'

'What? Were you worried I was ill or something?' Hugh laughed. 'You thought that I might only have a few months left?'

Bertie forced a smile across his face. 'Exactly, I was worried. I mean, after all that time.'

'I guess, also...' Hugh's eyes flashed up to meet Bertie's. 'We were inseparable throughout our schooldays. After all these years, I suppose I missed you.' He smiled and turned to head off.

'With the case – I'd like to do what I can to help,' said Bertie.

'Perhaps we should keep this secret, just for a bit longer. We shouldn't tell people that we're working together yet. There might be a chance that they'd say something to you that they wouldn't say to me.'

'Okay, sounds good,' said Bertie, opening the door to the building and stepping inside.

Hugh stayed on the footpath and watched the door close, but before it had fully clicked shut, Bertie wrenched it open again.

'Hugh? How are you getting home?'

Hugh turned, looking at the empty space at the end of the footpath. 'Yes, I see your point. I sent away the car I was going to take a ride home in.'

Bertie spoke with the voice of a stern mother. 'You can't go halfway across London at this time of night.'

'I suppose—'

Bertie cut him off. 'Stay.'

'I can think of a hundred good reasons why I shouldn't,' said Hugh.

'And I can think of one good reason why you should. I've got a very comfortable sofa I can sleep on; you can take the bed as my honoured guest.'

'Fine.' Hugh smiled as Bertie held the door open. 'Except, you won't be sleeping on the sofa.'

A confused expression flitted across Bertie's features. 'I'm not sure what you're suggesting.'

'I'll be the one that takes the sofa, obviously. You're doing me a favour.' Hugh pushed past Bertie in the small hallway, starting up the stairs.

'Yes, on the sofa,' Bertie said, deadpan. He released the door and it started to swing closed. 'That makes perfect sense.'

Bertie followed behind Hugh, heading up the stairs. 'It's the third floor.'

Behind them the lock of the door softly clicked shut.

Chapter Thirteen

13

The morning sunlight filtered into the small kitchen through the branches of the tree outside the window. The shadows danced across the worktop as the leaves moved in the breeze. Bertie's eye kept being drawn back to the bathroom, instead of staying focused on the scrambled eggs he was cooking on the stove.

On the other side of the flat, the door to the bathroom had been casually left ajar, revealing Hugh, who was leaning over the washbasin. He peered into the mirror as he carefully let the edge of a safety razor glide down his cheek, removing the last of the stubble and shaving cream.

Suddenly aware that the eggs were dangerously close to being overcooked, Bertie removed the pan from the heat and spooned the scrambled eggs onto the waiting slices of buttered toast. He carried the two plates over to the small table, setting them down carefully.

'Very nice,' Hugh commented as he emerged from the bathroom, clean-shaven and buttoning his shirt. 'I see you're a master of the French technique.' He smiled, nodding at the plates.

Bertie sat at the table, inviting Hugh to join him. 'Am I? I'm afraid I have no idea what the French technique is.'

'No, neither do I.' Hugh laughed before tucking in, hungrily devouring the breakfast and washing it down with a cup of tea. 'This is brilliant,' he said, between forkfuls.

Bertie chuckled.

'What?' asked Hugh, innocently.

'I don't know, this all seems remarkably domestic, doesn't it?'

Hugh laughed. 'We should have moved into digs together years ago; I don't know why we didn't.'

Bertie shrugged.

'Come to think of it,' Hugh continued. 'Why didn't we? We could have done once we'd left school?'

A heavy silence suddenly appeared between them, hanging there awkwardly. Neither of them wanted to be the one to break it.

Hugh finally spoke, doing nothing to relieve the tension. 'I suppose you went off to university and all that,' he commented, trying to shift the conversation in a new direction.

'Yes, I suppose that's it. We went off in different directions for a while.'

'Quite a while,' Hugh agreed. 'But that's all in the past, a lot of ancient history. Back together again now, though, aren't we? Friends, just like we always were.'

Bertie smiled, although it didn't quite come naturally. 'Just like we always were,' he repeated, quietly.

At that moment the sharp ring of the telephone pierced the silence. Bertie got up, thankful for the distraction, and crossed the room to answer it.

On the other end of the line was Alice's familiar voice. 'Bertie, I've hatched a plan.'

He smiled to himself, speaking tentatively. 'Go on...'

'I've invited John Tay over this morning and we're going to very subtly squeeze him for information.'

'We're going to subtly what?' said Bertie.

'Squeeze him,' she repeated.

'I see. Starting your own investigation, are you, Alice?' He shot a look in Hugh's direction, who responded by playfully raising his eyebrows.

'*Our* very own investigation, Bertie. You'll come over, won't you. To help me out?'

'In that case, I'll be over as soon as I can,' said Bertie, before saying his goodbyes and hanging up the phone.

Hugh rose from the table, pulling on his jacket that had been hanging on the back of the chair. 'Look, I'd better go too. Let me know how things go. While you are off working away on your investigation, I'll be off working away on mine. I'm going to visit Katherine Debenham this morning, but I think that's something I should do by myself.'

'Hugh,' Bertie said, a note of apology in his voice. 'About the past—'

'The past is in the past, Bertie. I think it's safe to say that a lot of time has gone by since then. I think we'd be wise to keep going forward rather than looking back.'

Bertie nodded.

'Look, do you want to meet up with me later on, after you've finished your investigation with Alice? I'm going to *The Era* offices this afternoon to see if I can find out anything more about this mysterious advert that was placed.'

'No one's owned up to it yet?'

Hugh shook his head. 'Not yet.' He headed along the short corridor towards the door of the flat. Before opening the door, he turned back to Bertie, who was still hovering at the other end of the corridor. 'If you do end up solving the murder with Alice this morning, you'll call me and let me know, won't you?'

Bertie smiled. 'You can count on it.'

Their status as official rivals meant that Bertie had never visited Alice at her home in Bloomsbury before. Whenever they did meet, it was usually somewhere out and about – neutral territory, you might say. Alice looked flustered as she wrenched the front door open and invited Bertie into her flat on the first floor.

'Oh, thank God. John is already here.' She stopped him in the hall and whispered, conspiratorially, 'To be honest with you, I didn't think he'd get here so quickly. I thought we'd have some time alone together so we could go over a plan before he arrived.'

'A plan? Do we *need* a plan?' he whispered back.

Alice rolled her eyes in impatience. 'Of course we need a plan, I thought you would help me to come up with one.'

'No, you're out of luck there I'm afraid.' He chuckled. 'Remember *you* were the one who invited *me*.'

'Yes, you're right, I did,' Alice said, directing her speech not in Bertie's direction, but in mid-air and to herself.

'Is that the dulcet tones of Mr Carroll I can hear?' came the soft Scottish voice of the director, out of sight in the next room.

'Yes, it's me,' Bertie called back. 'Shall we go through?' he whispered to Alice, who seemed to have frozen to the spot. 'Otherwise, he's sure to see through this brilliant ruse, whatever this ruse turns out to be.'

'Right, yes,' she replied when she realised that Bertie was looking intently at her, waiting for any hint of movement.

As the door to the main living space swung open, Bertie was rather taken aback at the chaos contained within. A large desk – at least he presumed there was a desk under there – was stacked high with books, scripts and piles of paperwork.

He thought about his own desk, which was usually empty except for his trusty Remington Portable and a neat pile of paper – the total sum of whatever he was currently working on.

The two contrasting workspaces seemed to be the physical manifestations of their personalities: one ordered, neat and methodical, the other an expression of boundless creativity that refused to be contained.

Alice noticed Bertie's look as he took in the scene in front of him. 'I know, Bertie. I don't suppose you would believe me if I said I tidied up especially because you were coming over.'

'Certainly, I would believe that this is tidy for you,' he joked.

Across the room, John caught Bertie's eye. A larger living space, which was rather less cluttered, with two sofas and a table was visible through an arched opening in the wall. The table had been laid out with tea. Bertie walked through and sat opposite him. Alice, still full of nervous energy, decided to remain standing.

'Alice tells me that you've teamed up together,' the director said.

Bertie shot a meaningful glance in Alice's direction before replying. 'Yes, I suppose that's what we're doing.'

'I think she's right though. I reckon we can get to the bottom of this ourselves,' John proudly stated. 'Between your two brilliant playwriting minds, you a specialist in murder mysteries and Alice in thrillers, combined with the added powers of me as director...' He leaned forward, speaking intently. 'We know the true nature of people, we put it up onstage every night. Real life should be no match for us.'

'I don't know if it's *exactly* the same,' Bertie replied.

'The trouble is that we creative types can let our imaginations run away with us.' He shot another look in Alice's direction, to emphasise his point. 'I think when it comes to the case of *real-life* crimes, your imagination can often work against you. I'm sure that in this instance, it's the cold, hard, boring facts that will lead us to a solution.'

John breathed out, relaxing back into the sofa. 'Perhaps you're right. I don't suppose you got anything useful out of that inspector friend of yours?'

Bertie shook his head. 'Nothing we don't already know, to be honest. There was only a small window where Anthony could have been killed. We were both at Romano's, along with Margo and Katherine, so none of us could have done it.'

'Yes, where were you?' Alice interjected.

Bertie knew that she had done her best to make it not sound accusatory, but she had only partially succeeded.

'Where was I?' the director replied, looking taken aback. 'I was in the office with Gareth the whole time.'

Bertie sighed. 'Unfortunately, I don't think we're going to solve this ourselves by finding out who was where when. There are just too many people milling about the place. It is a theatre after all.'

'You have to think, if it *was* an outsider, wouldn't we have recognised an unknown face amongst the crowd?' said John.

'I was an unknown face.' Bertie shrugged his shoulders. 'No one noticed me.'

Alice paced around the room, thinking. 'But

everybody knows who you are, it's not like you were a stranger.'

'Still, I shouldn't have been there. But there were lots of people there who wouldn't normally have been there,' said Bertie. 'Because of that advert. All kinds of extra people, daymen who some of the cast might not have come across, the police – although there were only a couple of them.'

'Yes, I see what you're saying,' said Alice, mulling things over. 'You think whoever placed that advert and the note did it in order to bring a bit of a crowd to the theatre? Not just in terms of bolstering the audience but making sure there were more people backstage as well.'

'Making it easier for an unknown face to blend in, if there was one,' Bertie added. 'It's a thought worth following. It is very easy to disappear; there's so much going on behind the scenes.'

John nodded in agreement.

'You didn't see who left the note?' asked Bertie.

The director shook his head. 'Sadly not, it was already there when I arrived. It's possible that it could have been left there the night before. It was only by chance that I checked for any post that morning – I don't usually get things sent to me at the theatre.'

'What did it say?'

'I can't remember exactly, although it was much the same as that bloody advert: *you have been warned – a murder will be committed during the third act of the play.*'

'It doesn't make any sense,' said Alice. 'Anyone

130

connected with the play would know that nothing of the sort happens. The opposite, in fact.'

'Tell me about Katherine and Anthony Debenham,' Bertie asked. 'You knew them personally; in fact, you knew them better than most.'

The director edged forward in his seat, leaning in before speaking. 'I don't know what there is to tell. Yes, I've known them for years.'

'You were very close to Katherine,' Alice noted, shrewdly.

'Yes, I always have been. I knew her long before she met Anthony. It was actually at some kind of gathering I'd organised when they first met – a party, a celebration of some sort. I can't remember what it was now. Love at first sight, would you believe – something I only thought happened in these plays of ours. But no, there was an instant connection between the pair of them. It was as if they'd been waiting their whole lives just to bump into each other.'

'Although, if we're to believe Margo Murray, it hasn't always been plain sailing,' said Alice, her disapproval of the journalist clear by her tone.

John's expression turned very serious. 'She got a lot more of it right than you might think...'

Alice's mouth opened, but the director clarified the comment quickly. 'Not that there was any infidelity, of course. But all marriages have their ups and downs, and that article coincided with a particularly rocky patch in their relationship. Anthony...' He stopped, not sure how to approach the subject.

'The gambling?' asked Bertie. 'Yes, we already heard about that.'

John looked relieved that he wouldn't have to explain the whole thing to them and nodded. 'Exactly that. They've managed to keep that side of things under wraps, except for a few close friends who did know, like me. Of course, there will always be rumours surrounding notable couples like the Debenhams. But, at the time, for those who were on the outside looking in, it's easy to see how the frictions between them could have been misinterpreted as infidelity. There were many people who did jump to that conclusion. She stood by him, though, and he pulled through.'

'With help from you too? You were there for support?' asked Bertie.

'Yes, of course. Like I said, we'd been close for years. Times when she felt lonely, abandoned... I was there to comfort her.'

'Yes, very close,' Alice murmured.

John wagged an accusing finger in her direction. 'Now, look here. I don't like what you're suggesting. I thought you'd asked me here so we could put our heads together, come up with something. If I've been brought here for some ulterior motive, to be accused, well... There's nothing like that between Katherine and me, not since—' He stopped himself from going any further.

'So, there was at one time something between you?' asked Bertie, encouraging John to clarify.

'A long time ago, years before she met Anthony. We were young, passionate, and yes, I believed for a time that it may have been love. But it wasn't. It was merely the inexperience of youth. We very quickly settled into a friendship and that's how it's remained ever since.'

Bertie did his best to phrase his question as delicately as he could. 'You've not been carrying a torch for her all these years?'

It was time for John's accusing finger to fall on Bertie this time. 'No. I've become just as good a friend to Anthony over the years – it's preposterous that I'd want to see him dead. There's just no reason. I care for them both very dearly, so I think you better stop asking these kinds of question before I say something I might regret.'

Chapter Fourteen

14

'She won't see you,' came a voice before the door had even fully opened. There was the merest hint of a French accent from the maid who stood in the doorway. 'She's resting, under doctor's orders, I'll have you know.'

No sooner than she had finished her sentence, the door began to swing closed.

'In that case, Miss...' Hugh left a gap, hoping that the maid would fill it with her name. She didn't. 'I'd rather like to speak to you and perhaps the Debenhams' driver, if he's around.'

'Well, in that case, you'll have to come in the trades entrance. I can't be receiving my own guests up here.'

The door was shut closed firmly before Hugh could get another word out. He stood there a moment, dumbfounded. His mouth had been open, ready to say something, but had been cut off. Instead, he settled for addressing the door with a polite nod. 'Thank you very much,' he said to the gloss black paint, shiny enough that he could see his own reflection.

He retreated back to the pavement and opened the iron gate set into the black railings. He followed the steps at the front of the house down to the basement, where he rapped on the door. In his opinion, it seemed to take a little longer than was necessary for the maid to appear through the frosted glass on the other side of the door. He wondered if she was keeping him waiting on purpose.

'Yes?' she asked abruptly, when she eventually wrenched the door open. She didn't give any indication that she recognised Hugh from their interaction only moments earlier. 'Can I help you?'

'A few questions, if you don't mind.' Hugh strode through the door and past her. He stopped a little way into the basement kitchen, finding a man standing across the room. 'The driver, I presume?' Hugh asked, judging by the man's appearance.

'Yes, that's right. Arthur Headly.' The man didn't offer a welcoming hand, keeping his arms firmly folded. 'What's this all about then?' he asked.

'I'm Inspector Hugh Chapman, I'm here to ask you some questions about the events that took place yesterday.' Hugh looked back at the maid, who was still hovering by the door behind him. 'Perhaps you might like to take a seat?'

'Yes, Elise,' said Arthur, calmly. 'Why don't you sit by

me?'

Hugh noted the first name of the maid that the driver had let slip. She walked over to sit in a chair that Arthur had pulled out from underneath the large, worn wooden table that was positioned in the middle of the room.

Hugh pulled a chair out for himself and sat down. Arthur elected to stay standing, hovering behind Elise protectively.

'Is there anyone else that works here?'

Elise shook her head. 'Not that lives in, no. There's a daily woman we have for the cleaning and a cook who comes in to do the lunch. They've both been here forever.'

'When did you start working for the Debenhams?'

'About two years ago.'

Hugh nodded, making a note of the facts in his notebook. 'And you?' he asked Arthur.

'A little longer.'

Hugh held his gaze until he elaborated further.

'Four years, perhaps. I don't really know.'

'You've always worked as a driver?'

Arthur nodded. 'Before this, you mean? Yes, I worked for a firm that supplied drivers for some of the theatres.'

'And that's how you came across the Debenhams?'

'Precisely. I had driven for all kinds of people, directors, writers, actors – and yes, for the Debenhams on various occasions.'

'Both of them?'

'Yes, although it was Mr Debenham who asked if I would be interested in working for them permanently.

I suppose he took a shine to me.'

Arthur had been talking enthusiastically, but Elise shot him a quick glance and his smile faded a little.

'And you, Miss...' Hugh left a gap for Elise to fill in her surname. This time he was relieved when he got an answer.

'Joubert. I got a job the usual way, through an agency.'

'You work as Mrs Debenham's dresser as well, on her shows?'

'That's right, whenever it's required.'

'Neither of you were acquainted with each other before coming to work here?'

Elise shrugged. 'How could we have been?'

'Can you tell me your experience of the Debenhams' relationship? What was it like?'

'How do you mean?' said the maid, giving Hugh a piercing look.

'I know that a few years ago there were some frictions in the marriage,' prompted Hugh.

'We weren't here "a few years ago", so we don't know anything about the past, Inspector. We can't comment on that.'

'They did have separate bedrooms,' Arthur suggested.

Elise cut in quickly. 'As many married couples do. Perhaps, if they had differing work schedules, it would be less disruptive to maintain separate rooms.'

'Their work schedules were quite different, at least in recent years, weren't they?' Hugh asked. 'I understand that until this play came along, Mr Debenham hadn't been in work for some time.'

'That's right,' Elise replied.

'That didn't cause any friction in their relationship?'

Elise shook her head, partly in response to the question but also apparently in disbelief that the Debenhams' relationship was being called into question.

'It's true that at times they could live quite separate lives, but I think that would show the strength of their relationship rather than the reverse.'

'You mean when Mrs Debenham had a role in a show and Mr Debenham didn't? While she was performing, where would Mr Debenham be?'

'Usually at his club,' the driver replied. 'Sometimes I would take them both in together; they might dine before a performance but usually it would be after. I'd drop Mr Debenham off at The Garrick Club, where he would spend the evenings while she was performing.'

'Then, after any performance, they would travel back together?'

Arthur nodded. 'Mostly, but there might have been times where they returned home separately. If Mrs Debenham was socialising after her show, say.'

'I see. How often would that be?'

The driver shrugged. 'Perhaps once or twice a week.'

'You would return here with Mr Debenham and go back to collect her later?'

'Sometimes, although occasionally she would arrange a taxi for her return.'

'The same was true the other way around,' Elise interjected. 'If Mr Debenham wanted to stay late at the club, we would return here earlier in the night and Arthur would go back and pick him up. But those were rarer occurrences.'

'Did the same thing happen while they were in the play? Does Mr Debenham go to his club after the show, say, and Mrs Debenham socialise separately?'

Arthur nodded. 'Yes, that might be the case some nights.'

'How was Mr Debenham's manner after an evening at the club?'

'He wasn't a drinker, if that's what you mean, Inspector,' Elise said, bluntly.

'I just wondered if there had been any hints of an altercation, perhaps. A disagreement with any of the other members?'

Arthur shook his head. 'No, nothing like that. There was...' His voice tailed off after a stern look from Elise.

Hugh gave a deep sigh. 'I must impress upon you the seriousness of this matter and how you must tell me the truth. Not some version of it, if you think that will protect your employers. The complete truth. This is a murder investigation and what you say here today might help us catch whoever did this, even if you don't think it's significant.'

'The Debenhams were both independent and at times they led quite separate lives,' said Arthur. 'They did things differently.'

'What did they do differently?' asked Hugh.

'I just mean in terms of their work. Mrs Debenham would often want to arrive early before rehearsals and stay late to greet fans or well-wishers after the show. Mr Debenham preferred to avoid any people waiting outside and would often leave by the front doors. We'd wait in the car until she was ready to leave. They were both very strong together and fiercely protective of each other.'

'They were very much in love,' Elise agreed with a nod.

'But there was one confrontation between the two of them,' Arthur started then stopped.

Hugh was unsure if he was waiting for his permission to continue or the maid's and indicated that he should continue with the story.

'It was one morning when I was driving the two of them to the theatre for rehearsals. Mrs Debenham spoke to Mr Debenham quite firmly. She seemed to think he might be falling into his old ways again.'

'Was that gambling or women?' Hugh asked, delicately.

'The gambling. There was never any hint of another woman,' said Arthur, who clearly thought the latter suggestion was ridiculous. Elise shot a look at Hugh indicating that she was in firm agreement.

Arthur continued. 'Some amount of money had gone missing or was unaccounted for.'

'Cash?'

'Yes,' said Arthur. 'It was kept in their safe.'

'What did Mr Debenham have to say about that?'

'He denied it, of course. He said he had no idea what she was talking about.'

'Do you think he was lying?'

'Perhaps,' said Arthur. 'I really have no idea whether he had spent the money on gambling, something else, or if he'd even spent it at all.'

'There was no sign of a change in his manner, maybe after these nights at the club?' Hugh asked.

Arthur shrugged. 'Well, I suppose there were times when he might leave the club seeming a little… Distracted, that's probably the best way of putting it.'

'Could that suggest, if he was gambling, luck wasn't going his way and he'd ended up losing the money? Maybe it finally got to a point where it was noticed by Mrs Debenham and she confronted him.'

The driver shook his head. 'No, that's not quite right. The change in his mood didn't happen until after Mrs Debenham confronted him. If he was losing money, he was very good at hiding it. But perhaps his mood only changed once he'd been caught out.'

'I see,' said Hugh.

'Mrs Debenham might have made a mistake,' Elise suggested in a hopeful voice.

'I understand she kept a pretty tight rein on the financial side of things. Do you think she could have made a mistake?

Elise shook her head. 'No, I don't think so. It was just a suggestion.'

Hugh nodded, thoughtfully. 'Perhaps the money could have gone missing for some other reason, especially if it was cash kept in the safe. Perhaps someone within the household took it?'

'You're saying it was one of us?' said Elise, sitting up a little straighter, offended.

'No, Miss Joubert. It was just a suggestion,' he said, repeating her own words back to her.

Elise looked over at Arthur and then back to Hugh. 'Well, the thought is quite ridiculous. Both of us are completely loyal to the Debenhams.'

'Yes,' said Hugh. 'That is quite clear.'

Chapter Fifteen

15

The floor vibrated under Bertie's feet as he clambered his way to the back of the bright red bus while it idled on Charing Cross Road. He hopped off the rear of the vehicle outside the Garrick Theatre. As the bus departed, leaving him in a cloud of petrol fumes, he was confronted with a poster bearing his own name. Well, half of his name anyway.

A cheery-looking man, holding a brush loaded with glue, was halfway through the process of pasting a large poster made from multiple sheets over the top of a hoarding for one of Bertie's shows that had closed the night before. The new advert announced the show that would be opening there next week. The man slapped up the last sheet of paper somewhat haphazardly, obscuring Bertie's name completely. He slid the sheet around in the wet glue, carefully lining it up with the rest of the paper sheets before giving the whole thing a final smoothing down. His work complete, he gave a nod of his head to Bertie, whom he had noticed watching him work, and set off on his way down the street.

Bertie stood there a little dumbstruck. He had found the whole thing quite disconcerting. He hoped that his playwriting career wouldn't be so easily papered over and lost to history, but he knew how quickly trends moved. The stars of today are quickly forgotten by tomorrow.

It made him think about Anthony Debenham and how quickly he had disappeared from the public consciousness. A decade or so ago, his name had been a big draw for audiences, but he soon fell out of favour. Whether that was what had brought on his gambling woes or if it was because of them, Bertie didn't know. It was a stark reminder of how easily replaceable people were in this business. The theatre industry could move fast and it was only a short hop from notability to: 'Remember so-and-so, who used to be in plays?'

He watched while some of the scenery was being loaded out onto the street by a team of stagehands. The door from the street to the stage was very tall and thin, and the large scenic flats – the wooden frames covered with painted canvas – could be slotted neatly through it. Any larger scenery had to be made collapsible in order to fit through this slender opening, otherwise it would have to be awkwardly manhandled through the front-of-house spaces where, after a great deal of effort, it would eventually reach the stage.

Seeing all the scenery stacked haphazardly against the outside of the building did little to alleviate Bertie's thoughts of how temporary and transient the world of theatre was. This was the end of the road for this play, at least for now. The scenery would probably go back to one of the many workshops south of the river, where the flats would be broken down into their component parts ready to be resized and rebuilt for a new set – that's if they couldn't just be repainted as they were.

Not wanting to keep Hugh waiting, he quickly set off. He passed down the quieter back streets and along Maiden Lane, behind the back of the Adelphi Theatre and the Vaudeville. No scenery was being loaded out of these theatres today and their stage doors were locked and deserted.

The world of theatre moves on a Sunday and Bertie wondered idly how many touring shows and their acting companies were travelling across the country at this very moment. They would leave their venue on Saturday night, travel on a Sunday and open again on a Monday evening in a brand-new town or city.

The idea of continually being on the move, upending your life once a week to traipse from digs to digs, made Bertie feel anxious. He very much enjoyed staying stable and settled in one place. A nomadic lifestyle did not seem compatible with him.

Bertie's thoughts and anxieties quickly faded when he turned into Tavistock Street and saw that Hugh was already there waiting for him. He disliked being late for anything, especially any meetings or rehearsals. It left him with the feeling that he was three steps behind everyone else. Once you found yourself in that position, it was often very hard to catch back up again. Hugh stood in front of an imposing facade, the entrance on a rounded corner of the building. A bold sign declaring *The Era Buildings* dominated the curved frontage.

Normally the building would be competing with the noise and bustle of Covent Garden market, with hardworking porters carrying towers of crates back and forth balanced precariously on their heads. As it was the weekend, it was quiet. However, the smell of cabbage and other unidentifiable vegetables still hung in the air.

Bertie smiled as he reached Hugh. 'You know there's not going to be anyone here on the weekend, Hugh? Maybe just a receptionist?'

'I think a receptionist is just what we need,' said Hugh, returning the smile.

They walked up the steps to the front door of the newspaper offices. Inside the entrance was a dimly lit room. As Bertie closed the heavy door behind them, the majority of the sunlight was immediately blocked out.

The soles of Hugh's shoes made a staccato tapping sound on the tiled floor as he walked across the entrance hall to a woman who sat behind a small desk.

He showed her his police warrant card. 'I'd like to get some details about an advert that was placed in this week's edition.'

'Certainly, Detective Chief Inspector. Would you like to follow me through?' The receptionist led them through to a larger room, full of desks but without any people. Once they were on the other side of the door she stopped. 'Wait here, please.'

She set off, scanning the desks as she walked away. Bertie distinctly got the impression that she wasn't quite sure where the required information would be located. Apparently, she had seen something across the other side of the room, judging by the soft 'Aha' that was audible with the discovery. She smiled back at the two of them, holding up a finger as if to say, *one moment, please*, and set off across the room.

Hugh leaned casually against the wall while he waited, turning to face Bertie. 'I assume you're a regular subscriber?'

'Of course, although I don't read it that closely,' he admitted. 'My secretary keeps them all. She collects them and has them bound together every few months, so she can look up any information at the drop of a hat.'

Hugh attempted to recall the name of Bertie's secretary. 'Miss Williams?'

'Yes, that's right. Gertie. I don't know what I'd do without her.' Bertie thought about his efficient secretary, who had been a dedicated fan of the theatre long before she came to work for him and an absolute asset now that she did. He was also not looking forward to the inevitable telling-off he would receive when she discovered he had got caught up in another murder mystery; her Trinidadian accent would always increase in strength whenever she voiced her disapproval.

Hugh gave a soft chuckle at the two rhyming names. 'Gertie and Bertie? That's very sweet, you know.'

Bertie watched as the receptionist veered off to the right and started looking in a long drawer which must have been filled with index cards. He recognised it easily. His own secretary had several of a similar sort that had hundreds of index cards filled with information and codes he was unable to interpret and navigate himself. The whole complex system allowed her to catalogue and cross reference all kinds of theatrical information as something of a hobby.

'Miss Williams didn't notice the advert in the paper then?'

'She probably did, though she didn't mention it. She seems to be able read the whole thing, cover to cover, in the time it takes her to walk it over from the letterbox to my desk. I suspect, like most of us, she assumed it was simply a publicity stunt, something to promote the show.'

The receptionist called back to the pair of them, across the room. 'Sorry, what was the advert regarding?'

'*Time To Kill*, Alice Crawford's play,' Hugh called back. 'There was mention of a murder at the matinee...'

'I see,' replied the receptionist. She returned to the job of flipping through the index cards, searching for the relevant one.

She emitted another soft sound of some sort when she located the relevant card. With a deft flick of the wrist, she removed it from the drawer, carried it back across the room and handed it to Hugh. He inspected it closely. She hovered nearby the inspector, as if she didn't want to let the card get too far away from her reach.

'There's no name, no contact information,' said Hugh, tapping the card with the back of his hand. He looked back at the receptionist, who hadn't realised he was looking for an explanation.

'Yes. No. Sometimes they don't leave any.'

Hugh smiled. 'You just take the money?'

'Well, we have got a paper to run.' She snatched the card out of Hugh's hand, inspecting it herself, interpreting the various numbers and letters that had been scribbled in the corner of the card. She pointed to the codes, explaining to Hugh what they meant. 'The date is just before the print deadline for that issue and this mark means they paid with cash. Anyone who places advertisements with us regularly would have an account. I remember this now...' she said, suddenly and without a change of tone in her voice.

'You took the booking?' asked Bertie.

'No, but I was here when he came in to place it.'

'He?' repeated Hugh.

'It was taken down by one of the other girls, but I remember it. He was a strange man. It was a strange advert, too, although we didn't really think much of it. But an advert like that for a show, we'd normally receive it by phone or letter. It was funny that they sent someone in to place it, even more so that he paid in cash. That's why it stayed in my memory.'

'Can you describe him?'

'He was very tall, with sunken eyes. Quite a striking appearance – gaunt I suppose you'd say. He didn't look the perfect picture of health if you ask me. Pale skin and you could see the receding hairline he was trying to hide under his hat. He could have been a stock character out of a Victorian melodrama, certainly he was old enough to have been in one. A sidekick or the villain's accomplice, you know the look.' She returned to the drawer and replaced the card.

Bertie turned to Hugh with a meaningful look and said in a low voice, 'I know who that man is.'

Hugh looked surprised. He turned his back to the receptionist and muttered, 'Well, don't hold out on me. Who is it?'

'I'm afraid I don't know that. It's just Alice and I saw someone of that description coming out of Gareth's office at the theatre yesterday.'

'You're sure?'

Bertie shrugged. 'Not at all, if I'm being honest. But it was a man who certainly matched that description, tall...' Bertie's words trailed off as he lost confidence in the idea. The man's height was all he had to go on really; he had swept by the pair of them so quickly. He had been tall, slightly skeletal-looking and had sunken eyes, just as the receptionist had described.

'Well, that's something to go on,' Hugh said, encouragingly.

'There was a heated exchange between the pair of them, too,' said Bertie, thinking aloud.

'What was it about?'

'Well,' said Bertie, hesitating. 'I said I wouldn't mention anything unless it became relevant.'

'Are you keeping things from me, Bertie?'

'No... But I did promise.'

'And has it become relevant?' asked Hugh, concerned.

'I'm afraid it might have done, yes.'

Hugh sighed, seriously. 'Well, don't think about it for too long. I don't like the idea of you keeping things from me.'

'I'll think quickly.' He smiled at Hugh. 'I promise.'

'Anything else I can help you with?' The receptionist's voice made them both jump a little. They hadn't realised that she'd returned and was hovering nearby, listening to every word they were saying.

'Thank you, you have been very helpful,' said Hugh, who had retrieved his notebook and begun taking notes. He paused in his writing and turned to Bertie. 'Have you had enough time to think about it yet?'

Bertie nodded. 'Let me tell you everything.'

Chapter Sixteen

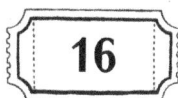

After a few sharp raps of the door knocker, someone eventually appeared at the door.

'Alice?' came a confused voice, surprised at the person waiting outside.

Alice took a breath before speaking. 'Margo. May I come in?'

'By all means,' she replied, stepping back and inviting the playwright inside. 'I notice you didn't bring your sidekick with you today?'

'He's with...' Alice stopped, halfway in through the door, her natural distrust of the journalist stopping her from revealing any more information than she had to.

'With his detective friend, is he?'

'You know what, Margo, I have no earthly idea.' Alice continued in through the door and strode past. She headed down the corridor and stopped at a half-open door. 'In here, are we?' she asked, before nudging the door open in curiosity.

'Yes, by all means, come in and take a seat.' Margo's sarcastic comment hung in thin air, as her visitor had already disappeared inside.

Alice chose a chair in the corner of the small living room although, as she lowered herself into it, she found the seat of the armchair was closer to the floor than she had been expecting. It caused her to collapse into it heavily and had the effect of coming across more dramatically than she had originally intended.

'Sorry,' she said. 'I'm glad to take the weight off, if I'm being honest with you. All morning I've been on my feet, pacing around my flat, trying to figure out this whole murder thing.'

'And have you?' Margo perched a little more delicately on the settee opposite. 'Figured it out, I mean?'

'No.' Alice looked around the room, taking the whole place in, trying to avoid the inevitable conversation that she knew she would eventually have to start. Eventually the silence could be held no longer. 'I've come to offer you an apology,' she said.

'Oh?' Margo sounded pleasantly surprised.

'Well, hold on a moment. It's a sort of apology,' Alice quickly clarified.

Margo laughed. 'Well, is it an apology, or isn't it?'

'There may have been a time, recently, where I might have suggested that you fabricated an article about the state of the Debenhams' marriage, insisting that the whole thing was a complete work of fiction.'

'Yes?' pushed Margo, encouraging Alice to continue.

'Now, there have been some new facts that have come to light. It turns out that perhaps there *were* some troubles in their marriage.'

'Oh, there were, were there?' asked Margo, unable to prevent a hint of smugness creeping into her voice.

'Let's not get too carried away. There were some troubles in their marriage, however they weren't caused by infidelity – as you suggested – but down to Anthony's habit of gambling their fortune away.'

'Right.'

'That's why it's only half an apology, because I was only half wrong. You were still half wrong as well.'

Margo smiled. 'I see, well that's very gracious of you, Alice.'

'Thank you.'

'Of course, it's all codswallop,' Margo exclaimed with a laugh.

'Margo, please,' Alice protested.

'It is,' she continued, uninterrupted. 'That article was a fair representation of what went on. Now I do admit that I might have leaned too much on the infidelity side of things when, as you say, that may not have been the full reasoning behind the breakdown in their marriage at that time, but who can blame me? Who cares if a rich actor loses all their money on the horses? Relationship woes are just the kind of thing that sells newspapers.'

'Yes, of course that's how your mind works. Even if there was some other woman involved, which I can't believe for a moment, in the end they reconciled. The way I see it, the kind of love that is developed and nurtured through years of marriage is far more potent than any infatuation from some "bit on the side".'

'That's certainly what it looks like, isn't it?' said Margo.

'But you don't think so?'

'I think that in reality, their relationship was much more along the lines of the feuding couple you wrote in your play, rather than the happily married couple they portrayed themselves as being in public.'

'I just find that unbelievable,' admitted Alice.

'They are professional actors, after all, both of them masters in deception.'

'That's not what being a professional actor means,' said Alice, grumpily.

'Well, that's a difference of opinion that we'll have to both live with, I suppose.'

A steely stare was held between the two of them for a moment, before Alice broke the impasse and shook her head. 'What I can't quite fathom is, if what you say is true, how on earth you knew about it? Especially when they were able to keep all their troubles hidden from the theatrical establishment at large. We all know how gossip spreads through the West End like wildfire.'

'Yes, Alice, we do. And you, the biggest gossip of them all.'

Alice huffed. 'I don't for a moment think that's true.'

Margo simply smiled in response. 'Well, we each have our own perceptions of ourselves, don't we? It might be more accurate to call them deceptions of ourselves. We all want to think of ourselves as better than we are.'

'And is your perception of yourself the same as what we all see? Someone who can write an article out of spite, tearing people down with a few quick-witted remarks?'

There was an awkward silence between them.

'Sorry, that was uncalled for, Margo.' Alice shifted in her seat sheepishly. 'I didn't really mean that, but it's just... Well, you often try my patience. That's all.'

'I'm not completely clueless. If you really don't think I know what people's opinion of me is, you're wrong. I do. As we're being frank with each other, it's simply my job to sell newspapers. It's something I do very well, by the way. We're both in the entertainment business, you and I, and that's what my stories and critiques of productions do. Sell.'

'I just don't understand how you – someone who people would be wise to keep at an arm's length from their personal lives – managed to find out something that no one else knew.'

'It is my job, Alice.'

'But there was not even a hint of it, something that no one else would have even believed...'

It was now Margo's turn to shift awkwardly in her seat, while Alice gave a deep, interrogating stare.

'Unless there was a direct connection,' Alice mused.

Margo sighed deeply.

'Wait,' said Alice, sitting a little more upright in her seat. 'Was there a direct involvement?'

Margo put up a hand in protest. 'Let me stop you there, before you get too excited and let your imagination run wild. Goodness knows, you playwrights do love making up fanciful tales.'

She paused, looking carefully at Alice, as if she was judging whether she should continue. As she began speaking, her normally hardened exterior softened a little. To Alice, she looked quite vulnerable.

'I think you're right, you know. What a turn-up for the books that is; something we actually agree on for once. The love that grows within a marriage is far more potent than any other kind. So, you have to understand, when Anthony was unfaithful it was when he was at his lowest ebb.'

'You were involved, weren't you?' said Alice, with curiosity. Margo didn't react. 'You and Anthony, that's it. That's how you knew.'

'I'm afraid so.' Margo let her head fall, providing confirmation.

'You didn't want to reveal that you were the girl on the side, so you pretended you'd received the information through someone else. But Anthony would have known, wouldn't he, that you were telling the truth about what was going on behind closed doors?'

'I was younger, Alice. More foolish back then. By the time I had written my article, it was already over between us. Anthony had – how shall I put it – come to his senses by then. The gambling, the affair. He wanted to put it all behind him.'

'And Katherine?' asked Alice.

'She was behind it all, I suppose. His recovery. When he finally came clean about it, she was there to help him through. As always, she was the perfect understanding wife. I'm not sure that she ever knew about me though, she thought it was just the gambling that had been the issue.'

Alice realised she had been holding her breath and took a gulp of fresh air as she digested the new information.

'So why write the article?' asked Alice. 'Jealousy, revenge?'

'A little of both, I suppose.' Margo looked at Alice with a forlorn expression. 'I'm not proud of it, you know. I never expected him to choose me over her. I'm not an idiot; I knew exactly what I was. But, yes. I was angry. I wanted to do something to show him how I felt. Betrayed. I know that sounds funny coming from "the other woman", but I did feel betrayed by him.'

Alice felt a little sorry for the journalist – genuinely and perhaps for the very first time. 'You must have known how it would end though. He would always go back to his wife, back to his normal life.'

'Just because I knew it would end, it didn't mean I wanted it to. So, I wrote the article as an attempt to expose him for the liar and cheat that he was. Perhaps that would be enough to finish them off. As you well know, that didn't go quite how I expected it to.'

Alice attempted a comforting smile, although she couldn't tell if she was doing it successfully. 'They always tell us not to believe what we read in the papers. I suppose it's ironic that the time we didn't believe it was the time it turned out to be true.'

'No one would believe anything said against the darling couple of the London theatre scene. After my article, they managed to keep everything out of the papers. The affair, the gambling, the lot. They have a lot of connections in high places. Katherine has always been very close with John Tay; he has a lot of sway in this industry. He was able to help them smooth a lot of it over.' Margo sighed. 'Of course, it didn't help me much either. By now, I should have been promoted, but there is still little or no chance of that. The paper has always been happy to keep me on as a writer, but any chance of moving up in the ranks are dead in the water now.'

She slumped back in her seat, her confession now over.

'Well, now I'm thoroughly confused,' Alice admitted, after a few moments' thought. 'Does this mean anything, in terms of the murder?' Her face changed. 'You?'

Margo laughed, although the sentiment didn't quite reach her eyes. 'You can't possibly think I could have had anything to do with it.' Her voice rose in pitch.

'Wouldn't you have had a reason? Some kind of jealous revenge?' Alice offered.

'This is what I mean about playwrights always look-ing for dramatic stories to tell,' Margo said, shaking her head. 'After all these years? I think not. It was a time in our lives that we both regretted, but it was also something that we had both moved on from.'

'I do have one question, though,' said Alice, slowly.

'Go on.'

'Katherine Debenham. You said she never knew about the affair? Never believed it, even when you wrote about it?'

'No. Not as far as I know. Even if she did believe that something had happened, I don't know that there was any reason for her to know that it was me.'

'It's just ... your long-running feud...'

Margo laughed, lightly. 'I wouldn't call it that. We were never going to be the closest of friends, of course. I would rather think that if she had known, she certainly wouldn't give me the time of day. But she would give me the occasional interview, the odd quote here and there.'

'I was just thinking,' said Alice. 'What if she had found out – would that have been a motive?'

'Perhaps, but it doesn't matter either way. There's no way she could have done it. Remember I was with her the entire time – when I met her at the stage door, when we went to get her coat, up and down in that silly little lift, and when we trotted down the Strand to Romano's afterwards. I saw that the dressing room was empty with my own eyes. Anthony Debenham was murdered by someone else. That is simply a fact.'

Alice seemed to ignore Margo's comments and continued pondering aloud. 'And if she did murder him because she'd found out about the affair, you don't suppose that you might be murdered next?'

Margo looked shocked; her mouth opened and closed a few times noiselessly before she composed herself. 'Well, thank you for that Alice, you've really made my day.'

Chapter Seventeen

17

Bertie enjoyed the feeling of the warm sun on his face. For someone who spent their days in a darkened theatre or typing away at a desk indoors, it felt like a rare treat.

Together, he and Hugh wandered down from *The Era* offices in the direction of the river, while Bertie explained to Hugh the details of the theatre manager's secret wager that he had placed on the show not completing its run. They had reached Victoria Embankment Gardens, which were relatively quiet, although every now and then you could hear the rumbling of Underground trains as they passed underfoot. The feeling was unsettling, as if the ground was moving beneath their feet. However calm and serene things appeared on the surface, the machinery of the city whirred away below.

It reminded Bertie of the theatre, where to the

audience everything would appear easy and effortless, with the engineering hidden away from sight, the wires, winches and mechanics working their hidden magic. Often the illusion was all too convincing. The Kirby wires that helped Peter Pan and the Darling children to fly had been so invisible and convincing it had necessitated that the playwright invent the concept of fairy dust, worried that some innocent child might throw themselves out of their bedroom window, merely thinking happy thoughts.

However, the machinery of the theatre is not just in the engineering, it is the people who become part of the theatrical machine: the dressers, crew, stage managers, all working together as synchronised as the parts in an engine to build the illusion for the audience.

As his ruminations on the people of the theatre faded, his thoughts turned to Hugh, who was now walking beside him in silence. Had it been anyone else, Bertie would have felt awkward without speaking for so long and would have felt obliged to make small talk to fill the emptiness. However, with him, the silence felt comfortable.

While they wandered, Hugh had been deep in thought as well. Like the trains rumbling under the gardens or like Bertie's musings on the theatre, his face gave very little indication as to what was going on underneath the surface. This, too, was an illusion of a man who was calm on the outside, but if you looked closely enough you could see the ideas rumbling underneath or the thoughts whirring away behind the scenes.

Sensing Bertie's gaze on him, Hugh turned and smiled, before stopping and sitting on a nearby bench. 'Connections. That's what I'm looking for,' he said, answering Bertie's unasked question.

'Between this man – the one who placed the advert and the same one we saw leaving Gareth's office – and the murder?' asked Bertie, sitting down next to him.

Hugh leaned forward in thought, his elbows resting on his knees. 'Between any of it,' he said, sounding a little irritated with himself. 'When it comes to crime – murder, particularly – everything leaves a trace. There is always a link or a connection, always something left behind to uncover. Most people who kill do so in a fit of passion – blind fury, if you like. It's not neat, it's not planned, it's messy.'

Bertie swallowed. Despite being the architect of dozens of fictional murders in his plays over the course of many years, he didn't have the stomach for the real thing. In his own writing, there was generally very little blood and any gruesome parts would occur offstage or hidden from view. In real life, it turned out, things were much more macabre.

'So, what are you saying, Hugh? This one was too neat?'

'Very. No mess, no destruction. Just a neat body, lying on the floor.'

'Right,' said Bertie, taking more effort than usual to remember how to swallow.

'There has to be some element of planning involved

and that always leaves links – connections between people. For instance, if drugs are involved to subdue a victim, they have to be bought or found.'

'Which leads us to who?' said Bertie.

'This man, who is new and doesn't seem to have any connections to anyone. Yet...' Hugh added hopefully on the end.

Bertie nodded. 'Except our theatre manager. We should ask Gareth James who he was, that's if he'd tell us...'

'Even if he doesn't, we have our ways.' Hugh smiled. 'Just based on a description, you'd be surprised. Certainly, if he's known to us or if he's had any dealings with the police, someone on the force will recognise him. They always do.'

'You sound confident,' said Bertie.

'You often don't have to look that hard. These people, they always surface somewhere again; they just can't keep away from a crime scene. The temptation to check on things is always too great. People want to see if they're getting away with it, find some information about the investigation. If there is a plan they have set in motion, they need to check that the plan is working.'

'And we're assuming there is a plan because of the advert; it was placed in advance,' Bertie said, pleased to be turning the conversation away from dead bodies.

'Exactly,' Hugh agreed. 'There had to be some forethought to this murder.' He sighed then stood up, although he gestured to Bertie to stay seated. 'There's a police box just outside, on Embankment. I'm just going to make a call. I suspect that a quick visit from a nearby constable will elicit a name from our friendly theatre manager in no time.'

Bertie nodded and Hugh swiftly departed. A light breeze rustled through the trees, gently rearranging Bertie's hair. Normally he was overprotective of his hair, taking great pride in styling it each morning. It would normally have annoyed him that his work had gone to waste, but that didn't seem to matter today. It was a perfect spring day, the type where it's bright and warm, but without the full ferocity of the summer sun.

A small dog trotted past, its short legs peddling away furiously in order to keep up with the brisk pace of its owner, causing Bertie to smile. As they passed, his eye was drawn by a movement just behind the Robert Burns statue in front of him. That wasn't just the movement of the foliage blowing in the breeze.

A sharp cracking sound as a branch broke was quickly followed by a swear word in a soft Scottish accent.

'Hello?' Bertie called in the direction of the bushes.

There were a few moments of hesitant silence before the hidden person decided there was nothing else to do but reply.

'Oh, what's the use?' came the reluctant Scottish voice.

'John?' said Bertie, as the familiar figure of the director emerged from the undergrowth.

'Now, I know what you're going to say...'

'Do you?' replied Bertie. 'Well, that's rather extraordinary, because I'm very much lost for words. What on earth are you doing in there?'

'Something that it turns out I'm not very good at, considering I've been caught. I've got to admit that it doesn't look too good, does it?'

Bertie almost wanted to laugh as John plonked himself down on the bench next to him, out of breath.

'Were you spying on us?'

'Well, yes,' John blurted out, quickly deciding that honesty was the best policy in this situation. 'I was just outside the theatre, and I saw the pair of you heading in this direction, so I sort of followed.'

'John!' Bertie said, in an accusing tone.

'Like I said, I know it doesn't look good. I just wanted to see if you'd found anything more out.'

'Well, why didn't you just stop us and ask?'

'Well, in hindsight, I'm sure there are a lot of things that I might do differently... But I didn't. I just thought maybe I might be able to overhear something.'

'So you hid in the bushes and listened in to our conversation?'

'I didn't hide,' said the director, trying to explain himself. 'It turns out that I just *happened* to be hidden over there. And I wasn't really listening in, because you cannae hear anything from back there anyway.'

Bertie gave a disapproving look. 'It's interesting really, because we were just having a conversation about how murderers regularly return to the scene of their crime.'

'Bertie!' said the director, in astonishment. 'What are you accusing me of?'

He smiled. 'I'm not accusing you of anything, just telling you what our conversation was about. Although interesting that you should take it as an accusation.' He let the comment hang there, halfway between a joke and a question, then said, 'You've been in and out of the stage door. Have you seen anyone hanging about?'

'Hanging around outside?' John thought for a few moments. 'No, I don't think so.'

Bertie slumped back onto the bench, hoping that Hugh was having more luck tracking down their mystery man.

'Other than the usual, of course,' John added.

That certainly got Bertie's attention, and he sat upright directly facing the director. 'What do you mean, apart from the usual?'

'Well, the usual collection of people that hang around the stage door. You know Katherine has a regular lot, I recognise quite a few of them from previous shows that we've done together. But, generally, there's always a few of the same faces you recognise across the West End.'

'And is one of them tall and sweeps around the place in a massive coat? Pale skin, sunken eyes—'

'With thinning hair on top?' asked John. 'Yes, I've seen him outside the Gaiety during our show. He's well known to people in the industry. I'd be surprised if you haven't heard of him. Shilling.'

'Harry Shilling?' said Bertie, the name bringing a faint glimmer of recognition.

'That's the one. You have heard of him, then?'

'Only by name, I don't think I've ever met the man. I've had no need to. But I know the sort of things he gets himself involved in.'

The two of them sat quietly for a moment, not sure what this revelation meant. Bertie knew it was now more important than ever to try and track down this mysterious figure.

'Hullo, hullo,' came Hugh's familiar voice as he approached the bench. Bertie thought that it was the most like a policeman he had ever sounded.

'Look who we have here,' said Bertie.

Hugh nodded a greeting. 'Mr Tay.'

'John followed us down here.' Bertie felt the director wince a little at the hurried summary of events, so he quickly continued, 'But that's not important. What is important is we think we know the identity of our new mystery man.'

'From Bertie's description of him, he sounds like Harry Shilling. I recognise him from previous shows, as well as this one. He's often found hanging around stage doors in the West End.'

'That's good.' Hugh nodded, taking in the information. 'It seems like the constable I've just dispatched to the theatre will have a wasted trip.'

'Do we think it could be him?' asked Bertie, with some enthusiasm. 'Could he be our murderer?'

'Well, let's not jump to any conclusions. First, what do we know about him?'

'Well, he's a shady character,' said John, 'that's for sure. He gets things for people, that's as much as I know. I'm afraid I don't know that much about him; I've never required use of his "services". But the rumours are he can get his hands on pretty much anything you might want.'

'Could he have been a fan of Katherine's?' asked Bertie.

'I don't know. He's a fan of the theatre though – you might say an obsessive fan.'

Bertie turned to Hugh. 'Does that mean something?'

'It does.' Hugh sighed. 'And it doesn't. Maybe there is some possibility that this mystery man is an obsessive of Mrs Debenham who killed her husband, a story of misplaced jealousy, perhaps. But there are other possibilities too. If this Shilling character is able to get his hands on anything, could he possibly have connections to the criminal world?'

'Is it possible?' said John. 'I'd say it's almost certain.'

'We already know he is the kind of man that would run a book, so there could have been some history with Mr Debenham there. Were there unpaid gambling debts he was owed? Scores to be settled? It opens things up a bit more. If he did have the right connections, could he have involved someone for hire, someone more professional?'

No mess, Bertie thought and shuddered.

Hugh continued, 'We'll have to look a little closer at Mr Shilling's past before we know what he's capable of.

But if he is some kind of obsessed fan...' He let the words tail off, thinking through the ramifications. 'If that's the case, then surely this mystery man will reappear in due course. If his intention was to get rid of the husband in order to pursue Katherine Debenham for himself, he won't stay hidden for long. Do you know where we might find this Shilling character?'

John shook his head. 'I'm afraid not. But he'll be around – he always is.' His expression changed quickly, having just processed Hugh's previous comment. 'Hold on a moment. What you said just then... You mean Katherine could still be in danger?' Without a moment's hesitation, he shot up from the bench and disappeared without a further word.

'Protective of her, isn't he?' said Hugh.

'Do you really think she could be in danger?' asked Bertie, echoing the director's concern.

Hugh was still, although Bertie could see that his mind was working quickly. 'Yes, at least...' He paused a moment, before looking Bertie directly in the eyes. His gaze was piercing. 'I think someone is in danger. I just don't know who.'

Chapter Eighteen

18

The sun had disappeared behind the clouds and was now refusing to come back out. There was a decided chill in the air as Bertie and Hugh left the quiet sanctuary of Embankment Gardens. No longer were the trains a soft rumble that came from underground, but loud mainline engines which clattered and rumbled overhead as they departed from Charing Cross Station.

They walked under the railway bridge and along Embankment as they headed for Hugh's place of work – Scotland Yard. It was only a short walk along the river but, as the wind swept down the Thames, what would have normally been a pleasant wander had turned into a minor ordeal. The air beat against their faces, and Bertie's hair – even though it had been perfectly arranged earlier – was now in complete disarray.

Over the years, Bertie had created several detective characters for the stage, both amateur sleuths and professional. He had taken care to make sure that none of them resembled Hugh, even though some of the stories that formed his plots had been inspired by letters that his friend had written to him over the years.

Because they hadn't seen each other in person since they were at school together, at least not until Brighton last year, he had never had the chance to visit Scotland Yard with him. He was intrigued to find out where all the police work happened.

As they approached the red brick building, with its bands of Portland stone stretching across it, Bertie thought it looked rather residential in a way. It was only when you took in the bottom half of the building, built in solid grey granite blocks, that it gave an indication that this was a place that meant serious business.

Sitting between the two buildings that made up the police headquarters were a set of large gates. Bertie followed Hugh through them and he led them in through a small side entrance. As they wound their way up the stairs a few people gave a nod of acknowledgement to Hugh as he passed, some even ventured a short 'hello' or 'afternoon' as they went on their way. None of them paid attention to, or even seemed to notice, Bertie.

They crossed a crowded room, full of people working at tiny desks in rows. The noise and chatter were quite intense and Bertie wondered how people could be productive in that sort of environment. During rehearsals at a theatre, he might be able to find a calm, quiet place to work in – an unused dressing room or in one of the empty bars – although peace was never guaranteed. A creative disagreement could quickly descend into arguing and, if the difference of opinion was large enough, raised voices could be heard throughout the building. Whenever he worked at home the only distraction was the muffled clicks of Gertie's typewriter coming from the next room. He couldn't work with the radio on or music playing, otherwise he'd end up having nothing to show but blank paper at the end of a day's work.

On the other side of the room, they walked into a smaller office. The sounds from outside filtered in but were muted and in here everything felt calmer. A number of tall filing cabinets lined the walls and two unoccupied desks faced each other across the room, both of which were stacked high with paperwork and other desk clutter. At the back of the room, positioned in front of the window, was a third slightly larger desk. Through the window you could see the river behind it. Hugh made his way around the desk and offered Bertie the chair opposite him.

Bertie sat down. 'Nice office.'

Hugh shrugged his shoulders dismissively. 'It'll do.'

Bertie was surprised to see that unlike the other desks he'd passed, Hugh's was kept neat and tidy, much like his own. There was next to nothing on it. All the paperwork was neatly contained in a set of wooden letter trays stacked five high. The only other object on the desk was an ashtray. Out of habit, Hugh opened a drawer to retrieve a cigarette and lit it.

'Those people...' Bertie jerked his thumb in the direction of the still-open door. 'Do all those people out there work for you?' he asked.

Hugh returned the question with a smile and a cloud of smoke. 'Most of them.'

Bertie took a surreptitious glance behind him. 'Do you think they think I'm a criminal?'

Hugh laughed. 'Why would they think that?'

'I don't know, the way I sort of got led in here?'

He shook his head gently. 'What we normally do is keep the criminals locked away downstairs. At the very least you should be in handcuffs.'

Bertie looked down at his wrists automatically.

'They probably think you're a witness, which you are,' Hugh said. 'Or maybe they think you're a grass. Tell me,' said Hugh, with the same piercing gaze, 'have you got any secrets you want to give up? Any criminal friends you'd like to turn in to save your own skin?'

Bertie smiled in return. 'Not today, thank you.'

Hugh pulled a folder from a stack in the topmost tray, dropping it on the centre of the desk and flipping it open. 'Statements from the theatre. All typed up and complete with spelling mistakes, I expect.' The typed sheets of paper were fastened together with a paperclip. He held them up one by one, as he sifted through the pile. 'Katherine Debenham, John Tay, Dennis – the young call boy – some guy called Bertie Carroll... He wasn't much use.'

'I don't know why I bothered,' joked Bertie. 'So, this is what real police work is, is it? You sit here comfortably behind a desk, flicking through those pages and finding the answers in between the lines?'

'Sorry to disappoint you, but nine out of ten times, yes. When you get everything together, look through it, find the discrepancies, you'll usually find that something doesn't add up. Being a good detective doesn't always mean being a man of action – a lesson some of my colleagues could do with learning. I'm sure that in your plays the police often are out doing dramatic things; that's more entertaining, after all.' Hugh took a long draw on his cigarette. 'However, I'm not in the entertainment business, so a lot of it is just this.' He picked a page up, scanned the text and let it fall back into place.

Bertie watched Hugh thoughtfully study each page, occasionally sucking on the end of the cigarette. He was a bit like a detective steam engine as he slowly emitted clouds of smoke. Bertie wondered if the rest of the detectives on the force would take such care and attention to detail. Perhaps they did.

Studying him in his place of work, Bertie realised there was something different about Hugh. Of course, there had to be. There had to be a reason why he had shot up through the ranks so quickly and become one of the force's star detectives. There was a reason why many of the most high-profile cases landed on his desk.

Hugh didn't just look the part, he acted it too. He was

every bit the tough guy you would expect of a policeman. Bertie certainly wouldn't have wanted to get on the wrong side of him. But seeing him here at his desk, unusually clutter-free in comparison to all the others around them, he didn't quite fit in. He seemed a lone rock of calm in the stormy sea that was the hustle and bustle of the building that surrounded him.

After taking a final draw on the cigarette, Hugh deposited it into the Bakelite ashtray. It dropped into the deep honeycomb pattern, disappearing from view. Even the ashtray was doing its part in keeping things neat and tidy. 'It all adds up,' he said with a sigh. 'No windows of opportunities, no gaps of recollection. No one saw anything out of the ordinary or saw someone hanging around suspiciously near the dressing room at the time the murder could have taken place.'

'Even though there were all those new faces in the theatre that day?'

'Well, yes. That does seem to complicate things a little, doesn't it?'

Bertie pointed to the typed statements, now spread about across Hugh's desk. 'But you said everything adds up.'

'That's the problem I have with all of it,' Hugh said, with a wry smile. 'It shouldn't. If we're getting a true and faithful account from everyone, it shouldn't. There's something in here that's incorrect; there has to be.'

'Does that make it any more likely that our new mystery man, Harry Shilling, is the murderer? Is he the link that we're missing?' asked Bertie.

'But he's so recognisable. Those features. There's no chance that he wouldn't have been seen by someone beforehand. Someone would have seen something. He could be the key though. If he's involved somehow, there has to be a connection there. Even if he's not our murderer, I just hope he can lead us to the answers we need.'

'Even if he's not our murderer?' repeated Bertie. 'So there's still a chance. You're not willing to rule him out completely?'

'I never rule anything out until I'm absolutely sure,' said Hugh, with a smile.

At that moment the phone, which was perched on top of a filing cabinet in the corner of the room, rang. He stood to answer it.

After a few murmured words into the handset, he replaced it and turned to Bertie. 'Harry Shilling,' he said with pride.

'What about him?'

'With any luck someone will be coming through that door with an address shortly.'

'You work fast,' said Bertie. He sounded impressed.

'Some of the bobbies recognised him from their beat, which strengthens our case somewhat.'

'It does.'

'Like I said, he's just too recognisable. If Harry Shilling had been inside the theatre yesterday, we'd know about it.'

Bertie nodded, wondering what their next step should be.

'Did we presume Mr Debenham's visitor was Danny Owen too quickly? Could Shilling have been the one who was visiting? Either way, I don't know if it makes much difference to events, as he was turned away.' Hugh shrugged. 'But it's interesting if it was him who tried to visit before the performance.'

'How about a disguise?' Bertie said.

Hugh shook his head. 'Disguises don't work in the real world, Bertie, not really. Fake beards and the like work alright up on the stage, when they're under bright lights and with some distance between the actors and the audience. In real life, up close, people see right through them.'

'But you have to remember this wasn't in the real world. It *was* in a theatre. Someone wandering around backstage, in a costume with a wig and heavy makeup, wouldn't necessarily stand out in that environment. In fact, quite the opposite is true. It might help them blend in.'

A small chuckle quickly turned into a tilt of the head as Hugh gave the idea some serious thought. 'Now that's a good point. Disguises in real life are often just too theatrical to be believable, but in a theatrical environment...'

Bertie did his best not to look smug about the compliment, but he could feel his face betraying him.

Hugh's focus was drawn to someone entering the

room behind Bertie.

A young policemen entered, handing Hugh a slip of paper which he studied.

'Thank you,' said Hugh as the policeman turned to leave. 'Wait a minute. Are you one of the lads who recognises him from your beat?'

The policeman stopped, facing Hugh. 'Yes, sir.'

'Do you know this Shilling character well?' asked Hugh, leaning back in his chair.

'A little.'

'Go on then, anything I should know?'

'Well, sir, he's a shifty character, that's for sure. Some minor theft, he's been caught running a book here and there, but he's never gone down for anything serious. We can never seem to get anything to stick.'

'And criminal connections, we think he has them?'

The policeman shook his head. 'Maybe some, but he's certainly not playing in the big league.'

'I see.' Hugh nodded his thanks to the officer, who subsequently turned and left without a word. Once he had gone, Hugh read the piece of paper in his hand again.

'What's that?' asked Bertie.

'An address. It's not quite what I was expecting if I'm being honest, but it's an address at least. Let's see if anyone's around...'

He lifted the phone receiver and dialled, reading the number from the slip of paper before passing the handwritten note to Bertie.

Bertie couldn't quite decipher the whole address from

the hastily scribbled handwriting, although he didn't have to. He instantly recognised the location from the first line.

Chapter Nineteen

19

The sun was hanging low in the sky as the police car sped over Westminster Bridge, taking them south of the river. Bertie had never actually visited the address that Hugh had handed to him, but it was a place that was familiar to anyone who worked in the theatrical industry.

There were a large number of workshops that built scenery for London's theatres and many of them were located south of the river. Several trades, like carpentry workshops, scenic artists and engineering firms, could all be found there. With reasonable rents and only a short hop over the Thames to the West End, it made it a very convenient location. The distance meant that the scenery never had too far to travel and, the majority of the time, would usually arrive unscathed from the short journey.

Joseph Harker – the name which Bertie had instantly

recognised at the top of the slip of paper – had died some years ago. His work as a scenic artist was well known and the studio he had run still continued under his name.

As the car pulled up outside the workshop, Bertie could see a small group of people filing out through a small door. It was set into a much larger wooden loading door and each person had to step over the bottom rail in the entrance threshold as they left.

'Looks like we arrived just in time,' Bertie commented as they got out of the car.

As they crossed the road, Hugh approached a woman who was holding the door open for the departing workers. She looked very much in charge.

'Detective Inspector Chapman,' he said. The woman seemed entirely indifferent to his presence. 'May we come in?'

She opened the door a little wider in invitation but didn't say anything as they stepped inside. Ahead of them, Bertie could see a storeroom piled high with large bolts of blank canvases, ready to be prepared, and hundreds of brown paper bags which were neatly stacked and labelled, containing dry pigments waiting to be mixed into paint.

She made her way up a long, thin and rather rickety-looking staircase. It led them up to the area that Bertie knew was called the paint frame – the main area of the studio.

'We've just called it a day, I'm afraid, so everyone's gone. Is it me you want to talk to?'

'Yes, Miss...?' Hugh let the gap hang there as a

question.

'Oh, Meredith Knight. They call me Merry, but I suspect that's a nickname laced with irony,' she said in a dry, husky voice.

The tiny staircase they had climbed up was positioned against one side of a much larger opening, used for loading scenery in and out of the studio. The finished painted cloths could be easily sent down to the floor below and out of the loading door onto the street. Protection from falling through this opening was provided by a thin and rather worn-looking rope, which didn't look like it would hold if someone actually had to put any weight on it. Bertie gave the perilous edge a wide berth as he and Hugh walked into the large space.

Even though the evening was setting in, the room was bathed in a soft, diffused light, thanks to the frosted glazing above them. The entire roof was glass, supported by thin iron beams. Cables and pulleys were strung between the beams; the whole effect gave the room an appearance that was almost cathedral-like. Large canvases, attached to the four wooden frames, were in various states of being finished. Some were nearly complete, others were sketchy charcoal outlines, a shadowy impression of the finished article that was yet to come.

The reason for their climb up to the first floor, and why the main studio space was located up here, was now clear. Each of the frames hung in a small slot in the floor. The pulleys and cables strung from the ceiling allowed them to be moved up and down by the artists using a series of counterweights. Posting the large frames, like letters, through the floor meant that the scenic artists could work on an entire canvas from a comfortable, standing position on the workshop floor, with easy access to all their paints and brushes.

There was a faint animalistic smell that hung in the air, something that was akin to a wet dog. Meredith saw Bertie's wrinkled nose and smiled. 'Ah, yes. I forget about that. You get used to the smell after a few years.'

'What is it?' asked Bertie.

'Animal skins. It's what we boil up to make the size which we use to prepare the canvases and make the paints.' She pointed to a tray of water on top of a gas burner.

Even though the burner had already been turned off, the water was still steaming. A collection of repurposed metal pots and old tin cans sat in the water.

'Mix it up with some pigment and you're ready to go,' she explained. 'It needs to be kept warm continuously, though. That's what keeps it liquid so you can paint with it.'

Bertie looked around the room and saw similar trays dotted around in front of the work in progress.

'I take it that you didn't come all this way to talk about paint though, did you?'

'I'm afraid not,' said Hugh. 'Do you know a man called Harry Shilling?'

'Now why would you ask me that?' Meredith wondered aloud. 'Yes, I do know a Harry Shilling, as it happens.'

'This is the address we have for him,' Hugh explained.

'That makes sense. He works here, humping and lugging things around the place mainly. He quite often spends the night here too. We have a few rooms out back for that purpose. It's not the Ritz, but it does the job.'

'He lives here?' asked Bertie.

'I couldn't say, to be honest. I don't know if he has another place. Like I said, he stays here most nights; one or two of them usually do when we've got a lot of work on. But he's not here all the time, so I suppose that means he must have somewhere else to go. I don't mind having people stay here; it's a bit of added protection against someone breaking in or the place burning down, isn't it?'

'When was the last time you saw him?' asked Hugh.

'I don't know. Not today, anyway.'

'Think harder,' pressed Hugh.

Meredith looked a little taken aback at the rebuke. 'I wasn't here yesterday – we don't normally work the weekends, it's just we're a bit behind with a few things. Thursday. I saw him on Thursday; we were loading out a few cloths so he would have been helping with that. Like I said, humping and lugging things for me.'

'Okay,' said Hugh, although he didn't sound convinced.

'He definitely hasn't been here today.'

Hugh nodded as he jotted everything down in his notebook. 'Fine, that's fine. Do you mind if we take a look at these rooms?'

'By all means, help yourself. Up there, to the left,' she said, jabbing her thumb to direct them. 'Can you manage by yourselves? I need to finish closing up.'

She didn't wait for an answer before setting off down the stairs and out of view. Every now and then some kind of banging or clanging could be heard as she busied herself with her duties.

'Shall we, then?' asked Hugh, indicating that Bertie should lead the way.

A long staircase rose diagonally across the back wall into the apex of the roof, where there was a small door. Bertie climbed up and disappeared through the opening with Hugh following. The two rooms that they found at the back would be more accurately described as two large cupboards. Each one had a couple of camp beds crammed inside, although only one of them looked like it had been used recently. The grimy windows let in a smudge of light.

Meredith had been right: there really wasn't much to look at aside from a pile of blankets. Everything looked in slight disarray, as if Shilling had just upped and left without any warning.

Hugh lifted some of the blankets and looked under the beds. 'There's not really anything for us to find here, is there?'

'It doesn't look like it,' said Bertie idly pulling open a small drawer. 'Just a minute, what's this?'

He pulled out a sheaf of papers; each sheet was filled with pencil sketches. Actors, actresses and theatre buildings were artfully drawn on each page. He showed them to Hugh.

'Anyone you recognise?' asked Hugh.

Bertie nodded his head. There were plenty of people he did recognise. Friends, people he'd worked with on shows over the years, were all represented here.

'This one seems particularly relevant,' Bertie said, holding up a page so Hugh could see it clearly. 'Katherine and Anthony Debenham, I presume.'

It was a drawing, outside the stage door of the Gaiety. It showed the married couple entering the building; Anthony held the door open for his wife. In the sketch she gave a wistful glance over her shoulder at someone or something that wasn't rendered in the image. She looked composed and elegant, whereas Anthony seemed to have a scowl across his face.

'They're good, aren't they?' said Hugh, reaching out to take the drawings from Bertie.

'They look it to me,' he agreed, although Bertie would be the first to admit that neither he nor Hugh were particular experts in the field of art. However, the drawings had been done with what seemed like a light and elegant touch. 'And recent,' he added. 'These ones must have been drawn in the last twelve weeks, if they were during the run of Alice's show.'

Hugh leafed through the drawings 'I don't know that it tells us much though, other than Mr Shilling is good with a pencil. With such artistic talent, I wonder why he's only used here as a labourer?' He turned, hearing a noise outside the room.

'Colour blind.' The explanation came as Meredith stepped into view in the doorway. 'He can't match colours. We can still use him for certain jobs, doing the underdrawings to work on top of. But most of the time he's useful for moving things around. He's a tall man: he can reach things that are high up.' She gave a shrug as she stepped into the room, carrying a large overcoat. She hung it on a hook next to the camp bed.

'I found this downstairs,' she said, when she caught the pair of them looking at her with interest. 'It was where everyone else hangs theirs.'

Hugh immediately set about searching the pockets. From one of them he produced a small piece of paper, which he inspected with a curious expression on his face. 'This is Shilling's coat?' he asked.

Meredith nodded her head. 'Yes, I'm sure of it.'

'Then this is certainly an interesting development,' said Hugh, passing the note to Bertie.

He looked down at the words typed on it. They precisely matched the wording of the advert that had been placed in the newspaper.

When Hugh handed the note to Bertie, it had been accompanied by an enthusiastic expression. Now it was Bertie's turn to return the look but instead, his was of confusion.

He had no idea what this meant.

Chapter Twenty

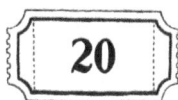

20

An ominous twilight hung over the scene as they departed in the police car. Bertie insisted he was dropped at the nearest Underground station, even though Hugh had offered to drive him all the way home. Hugh was taking a late-night visit to the Fingerprint Bureau at Scotland Yard, to see if he could get the note tested for what he kept calling "latent impressions".

He had mentioned something about a process called iodine fuming, the finer points of which Bertie hadn't quite caught, but he made a point of remembering the phrase in case it came in useful for one of his plays in the future.

Hugh set off in the car and Bertie, rather than entering the station and descending underground, hovered outside the yawning entrance. Hugh kept saying the answer was in the connections, but Bertie was struggling to find a connection between anything. Quite the opposite: all the various pieces of the puzzle seemed to be decidedly unlinked.

In his murder mysteries, characters always had a purpose. Every time someone walked on the stage, you could safely assume that there was a reason for them being there. Real life, of course, wasn't a play; it was much more complicated. Maybe it was entirely a coincidence that an incriminating note had been found in Harry Shilling's pocket. No, Bertie wasn't even convincing himself of that idea.

The bright electric lighting inside the station spilled out onto the pavement, as if it was extending a warm hand in invitation, but Bertie hesitated. The thought of going back to his flat on his own gave him pause. His thoughts returned to Harry's makeshift bedsit and he wondered whether he was a lonely person. Standing on the pavement he watched a few of the last evening commuters disappearing into the Underground station. Excited theatregoers or couples seeking other entertainment emerged onto the street. Suddenly he found that he wasn't quite ready to return to his empty home.

Instead, he decided to step into a nearby telephone box and placed a call.

'Alice. Sorry, I hope I'm not disturbing you?'

'Bertie! Where have you been? I called you earlier, but there was no one there. I assumed you were still out investigating. Tell me all about it. I want to hear everything!'

Hearing her exuberant response made Bertie smile. It was like receiving a warm hug down the telephone line.

'Would you like to do it over a drink?'

Bertie laughed at how enthusiastic her response was. 'Would I!'

Not more than twenty minutes later, the playwriting duo were descending the narrow steps down into Betty's. Unusually for Bertie, who didn't particularly like small, enclosed spaces, he found comfort in the room, which was crammed full of people and smoke.

The eponymous Betty stood behind the bar, wearing a perfectly tailored white tuxedo and a top hat. She welcomed them in with a smile as they made their way across the room to a table in the corner.

This was a bar for those who wouldn't fit in elsewhere. In advertisements the place was described as having a Bohemian atmosphere, but that was merely code for those in the know.

'How are you feeling?' Alice asked as they waited for the young server to come over and take their order.

'Questioning everything.'

'Everything? Well, that seems like a lot. I'm sure I can help you get to the bottom of it all.' Alice returned the smile of a young man who arrived at their table, waiting eagerly to take their order. She entered into a conversation about whisky with him, very few words of which Bertie really understood. 'What can I get you? Highland, Speyside, Islay?'

'You know I never really know the difference,' he admitted.

Alice tutted and smiled. 'Well, I suspect you're a Speyside man,' she said, giving the waiter a nod. She settled herself in the comfortable chair as he departed to fetch their drinks. 'It looks like you've had quite a day since you left this morning.'

'It's hard to know where to begin,' pondered Bertie. 'I don't feel like things have moved much further on from what we already knew. Although we're now pretty certain that the advert was placed by a man called Harry Shilling; he works down at Harker's.'

Alice tilted her head slightly. 'Well, that's progress.'

'The tall man we saw coming out of Gareth's office yesterday, remember?'

'Yes, of course. Shilling. I recognised the name, but didn't really know the face that went with it. I've never needed to cross paths with him, but one hears all sorts of things,' said Alice. 'I wonder why on earth he is involved in the advert; I suppose he's happy to do anything in return for money.'

'Yes, the why still seems a mystery. But the text of the advert was typewritten on a slip of paper we found in his coat pocket.'

'Did he own a typewriter?' Alice asked.

'No,' said Bertie. He felt a little taken aback that he hadn't thought of something so obvious. 'There wasn't one up in that room anyway.'

'Someone must have given it to him, so that he could

place the advert on their behalf.'

'I suppose that would be a logical assumption.' Bertie wondered why Hugh hadn't offered a similar theory at the scenic studio. Presumably it had been so obvious he hadn't thought to mention it. 'Hugh's taken it to get it tested at Scotland Yard.'

The waiter returned with their drinks. Taking a sip, Bertie found the subtle honey and vanilla flavours pleasant and the warmth of the alcohol soothing. 'You're right, Alice,' he said. 'I am a Speyside man.'

Alice put her glass down on the table, continuing where they had left off. 'The Fingerprint Bureau. Yes, I visited there once. A little background research for some play or other. Would you believe there are people out there in the world who have criticised me for not putting in enough effort to make sure the facts are correct in my plays?'

Bertie shifted awkwardly in his seat. 'I'm not entirely sure, but I'm afraid I may have been one of them.'

'I'm sure you were,' she said, with a look of pretend shock which grew into a mischievous smile. 'You know I find realism such an inconvenience sometimes. It always gets in the way of a good story. Anyway, I spent a morning there with a very excitable gentleman who insisted I should be calling them finger-marks and not fingerprints.'

'He's the expert, after all,' said Bertie.

'I said, if I did that, no one would know what on earth I was talking about. Audiences only know the terminology they read in their newspapers; it doesn't matter if they're correct. He also told me something very interesting: the lack of fingerprints can often be just as important as the finding of them. Of course, I thought that was very good, so I put that into the script right away.'

'You mean, if they've been wiped off?' asked Bertie.

Alice nodded while taking a sip from her glass. 'I'm sure it turned out to be a very good play in the end. If only I could remember what it was called or who was in it.'

Bertie smiled. 'I'll ask Gertie, she always knows.'

'Ah, that wonderful secretary of yours; she really is a marvel. I've never been able to get on with one. They always try to organise my time and schedule me like a machine. How can anyone work to a timetable like that? It's ridiculous.'

Bertie busied himself with his own drink. He didn't want to comment, but his working practices were entirely opposite to Alice's. A regimented schedule was something that suited him perfectly.

Onstage a woman accompanied by a piano player sang a plaintive kind of song that he seemed to recognise but didn't know any of the words to.

'Also, we were followed,' he said, remembering it suddenly.

'You're joking!'

'I'm doing this in all the wrong order. Yes, John Tay followed us. He said he saw us passing by the theatre, which seems like an incredible coincidence. I caught him hiding in the bushes when Hugh and I were in Victoria Embankment Gardens, trying to listen in on our conversation .'

Alice couldn't help but laugh at the image of the director emerging from the undergrowth. 'And was he able to overhear anything worthwhile?'

'I have no idea. I don't think there was anything useful he could have gleaned from our conversation, but it strikes me as suspicious.'

'It's certainly a strange thing to do, but then I've always found directors a little odd.' Alice sat up a little straighter, which he recognised as a sign that she was about to reveal a piece of salacious gossip. 'Margo was having an affair with Anthony Debenham,' she blurted.

'You're joking!' It was Bertie's turn to voice his surprise.

'That's how she knew for certain there was something going on in their marriage. It was Margo – *she* was the something. Imagine her crammed into that little lift with Katherine Debenham when they stopped back at the theatre. Margo must have nearly exploded with awkwardness.'

'I don't believe it,' he said, taking another sip from his glass.

'Right from the horse's mouth.' Alice smiled. 'This is all such fun, isn't it?'

He gave a deep sigh. 'I don't know about that. Anthony is still dead and we don't seem to be much closer to finding out who did it. This is what I mean about coming to question everything. I don't know that it is fun at all.'

Alice gave him a serious look. 'This is what we do, Bertie. We take our pain and reuse it for other people's entertainment. It's our job. Take all this in, write it down, put it in a play. Although, detectives and murder mysteries... That's more your area than mine, I must admit. Let me get my teeth into a thriller any day.'

'You can't escape it, can you? Everywhere you go, you end up turning people you meet into characters and imagining stories for them. Even on the way over here, there was something I made a note to remember. Iodine and fingerprints. I thought I could use it in a play one day.'

'And so you could,' agreed Alice, pointing her finger at him. 'And so you should. It's the little details like that which keep audiences coming back to your shows. "Great writers steal" – it's a quote that I can't quite recall, said by someone I don't quite remember.'

Bertie put his glass down on the table in front of him. 'It was different when I was taking things from Hugh's letters. Odd things he wrote to me about cases over the years. When they were written down, they were just stories. That felt different.'

Alice shrugged, noncommittally.

'But when you're actually involved... The idea of taking something from an awful situation like this – and it is awful – and repurposing it for entertainment...' Bertie let the words trail off.

'Lost your stomach for it, have you?' Alice asked, with a serious expression.

'I'm really not sure.'

'Well, you've never tried your hand at farce, have you? Maybe it's time you gave that a go.'

'I don't know that I'm quite in the mood for that sort of thing right now,' said Bertie, smiling. He picked up his glass and relaxed back into his chair.

'No, I was never that good at it. Do you remember that one I did at the Aldwych a few years back?' she recalled. 'I ended up having so many different rooms for people to go in and out of, the set ended up being more door than it was wall.'

Bertie chuckled. 'I heard about that one. Sounds like what was going on backstage was far funnier than what was going on in front of the audience. You should have put that in a play.'

'Yes, I'm afraid it probably was; what was going on onstage was really quite dreadful. It didn't help that the leading man was also producing the damn thing. He was so distracted by the process of getting everything up and running, he didn't get round to learning his lines until the second week of performances.' Alice ran her thumb along the rim of her glass, posing her question delicately. 'This Inspector Chapman?'

'What about him?'

'How did you two meet?'

'Old friends from school,' he replied. 'I hadn't seen him for years, not until Brighton.'

'Old friends,' Alice mused. 'I suppose you have plenty of stories to tell about him then.'

'I do,' said Bertie, holding up his glass. 'I'd need a few more of these before I'd be ready to tell them to you, though.'

Alice gave a knowing look, speaking seriously. 'We're spoiled as playwrights, you know.'

'What do you mean?'

'We always have such high expectations, which the real world can never quite live up to. We play God with our characters, deciding whether to give them their happy ending or not. We can always make them say what we want to hear. Unfortunately, that's not something we can do in real life.'

Bertie smiled. 'No, I suppose not.'

'Now, I'm older than you — ever so slightly — and I know I'm certainly wiser,' she said, with a chuckle. 'So, take this as advice or ignore me completely, it's up to you. When it comes to your own life, don't try to write your ending ahead of time. It'll stop you seeing things as they really are.'

'You think I've already written my own ending?' asked Bertie, sounding a little defensive.

'I'm just saying, always make sure you're making decisions based on what's really in front of you, not your idea of what you want to be in front of you.'

Bertie nodded and swallowed. 'I know.'

'With that said, let's drink to us.'

Chapter Twenty-One

21

A throbbing headache greeted Bertie when he woke in the morning. Before emerging from his bed with great effort, he swore to himself that he would stick to more familiar drinks in future.

After wrapping a dressing gown around himself, he set off towards the kitchen with the idea of putting the kettle on to boil. A quick glance at the hallway clock told him that he had exactly thirty minutes to make himself presentable before Gertie was due to show up and start work. In the five years she had been his secretary, he had never known her to be late for anything.

He started to make his way across the hall, but then stopped. Half a thought had occurred to him in his half-awakened state. He directed his feet not towards the main living space, but down the corridor into his secretary's office. He felt strange opening the door in his half-dressed state. Even though this was his home, this room was all business and he rarely ventured into it when Gertie wasn't there. This was her domain and she was in command of it completely.

Lining the walls were cabinets of all shapes and sizes. On top were several trays with a week's worth of correspondence sorted neatly into each one. Anything requiring attention would be marked up and put on Bertie's desk. Then, once what was required of him had been done, it was returned to the trays where it would either be posted or enter the complex filing system to be stored for future reference.

Luckily, what he was looking for was recent enough that it was still sitting in one of the trays. He rifled through them, risking his secretary's wrath for disturbing things. He pulled out a small typewritten note with a cutting from a newspaper clipped to it. He tossed it down onto her desk, letting it lie there incriminatingly. He sighed deeply.

Slowly, he lifted the receiver on the telephone. There was a slightly odd feeling hanging over him, like he was in one of his plays. It was a number that was easily recognised by theatregoers and was often called by actors during a play, including in many of his own. He remembered that a few years ago the number had changed, meaning playwrights would have to change it in their scripts, too. The number used to be Victoria 7000 but now it was Whitehall 1212 – the number for Scotland

Yard.

After talking to an operator, Bertie was surprised to hear Hugh's voice come on the line. He hadn't expected him to be at his desk so early in the morning, although he was relieved that he was. The sound of his friend's voice always gave him a sense of calm reassurance.

'Bertie, you remember that piece of paper with the advert typed on it that was found in Harry Shilling's coat? We can be sure of one thing – the fingerprints match the ones on that letter opener that was used to kill Anthony Debenham. The only problem is that we don't know whose fingerprints they are yet. We're assuming they're Shilling's, but we have nothing on file for him, so we can't be sure.'

Bertie looked down at the newspaper cutting on the desk and picked it up, inspecting it closely through squint-ed eyes. 'If you want evidence, I think I've got some right here.'

'Whatever you have, bring it to the theatre. Meet me there and we'll get everything tested for finger-marks, just like I did with the advert. Handle it carefully, though. Try not to touch it too much.'

Bertie dropped the newspaper clipping like it was a hot coal, hoping that the impression of his own fingers on the paper hadn't done too much damage.

'See if you can find some way of protecting it. Can you get it into an envelope? Who do you think it is?' Hugh asked down the telephone line.

'I'm afraid I'm now sure who typed that advert, but it

doesn't make sense to me at all. I'm looking at it with my own eyes; it's right here on paper, in black and white. I think it could be Alice.' Bertie swallowed. 'No, I'm almost certain it's Alice.'

The sticky ink on Bertie's fingers was difficult to rub away, but eventually the last remnants of it were gone. His handkerchief, however, looked a little worse for wear. It was covered in black smudges and as he stuffed it back in his pocket he wondered if the ink would ever come out.

'So, am I in the clear?' he asked.

Hugh was sitting next to the desk in the theatre manager's office. He inspected Bertie's fingerprint card and compared it to several photographs of the advert they had retrieved from the paint studio. Each image, produced by the experts at Scotland Yard, was of an enlarged section of the paper where clear finger-marks were present. After a close look at the pictures, he dropped them back on the desk and smiled. 'It looks like it, although we'll have to see what the experts say.'

Gareth James sat behind his desk writing numbers into a large ledger with a speed of mental arithmetic that Bertie, who was watching on, didn't think he would be able to manage. He didn't seem to be paying much attention to the detective and the playwright, who wouldn't normally have been sharing the room with him. He got up and left the room to attend to some business elsewhere in the theatre. He seemed so distracted by his work, he didn't even glance in Bertie or Hugh's direction as he left.

'What makes you think it was Alice?' asked Hugh, once the theatre manager had gone. He nodded his head in the direction of the wall and the room next door, where she was currently having her fingerprints taken by the same policeman who had just attended to Bertie.

'The typewriter she has is the same as that advert, the same as my own in fact. That typeface is recognisable enough when you spend every day using it.'

'Well, that's very impressive,' commented Hugh.

'Not only that, she has a damaged E on hers and you can see how it matches exactly.' Bertie pointed out the features in the photograph and on the note from Alice that was laid on the desk, being careful not to touch it this time. 'She's never bothered getting it repaired.'

'That does seem incriminating,' agreed Hugh. 'The broken E only features on the advert; the note that arrived the day of the show doesn't have it. The typeface doesn't quite match either.' He shuffled the photographs, comparing the two notes side by side. He held them up to illustrate his point, before throwing the whole lot down on the table, a little perplexed. 'Why on earth does she send you typewritten notes attached to terrible reviews?'

'We've been doing it for the last few years. Alice started it, I think. In fact, I'm almost certain that she started it.' Bertie chuckled. 'We find the worst reviews we can of each other's shows and send them to each other. I didn't like it at first, I don't really like to read the notices from my own shows, but this made it into a game.

Somehow it makes it all the more bearable.'

'And the note from Alice? *This reviewer is right, you've written an awful play, yet again,*' said Hugh, reading from the note that was waiting to be taken for analysis at Scotland Yard along with Alice and Bertie's fingerprints.

'That's quite tame for her, if I'm being truthful. She normally takes her time to craft a particularly cutting insult.'

'No, I mean, why does she typewrite them?'

Bertie laughed. 'I once joked about her handwriting and how it was basically unreadable. I said, if she was going to take time out of her day to insult me, at the very least she should make it legible enough to be read. She's been typing them ever since, probably out of spite.'

'The things you playwrights do to pass the time,' commented Hugh, dryly. 'It does only tell us part of the story though – that Alice's typewriter was used to write that advert; it doesn't necessarily mean that she was the person who wrote them.'

Bertie sighed. 'Yes, I did wonder that.' He sat next to Hugh. 'There is one other thing. You see how the letters on the advert have double printed, on the other note too.'

Hugh looked closely at the photograph of the note. Each letter had a ghostly impression printed alongside it. 'I know you're my theatre expert, Bertie, but maybe I should consult you as my typewriting expert as well,' he said, sounding impressed.

'I think you'll find that it's Gertie who's the typing

expert. She's pointed out an embarrassing number of faults in my typing technique over the years. This was done by someone who isn't an experienced typist. Whoever typed this was holding down the key for too long; it causes the hammer to bounce and double-print.'

'And we believe Alice to be an experienced typist?'

'Yes, of course. I expect she types for several hours most days. That might be the one thing that puts her in the clear. It doesn't appear in the notes she sends me.'

Hugh thought carefully. 'I don't know that we can rule her out or in. She just as easily could have typed in this way deliberately to draw the attention away from her.'

Bertie looked at Hugh. 'Yes. I was worried you might say something along those lines.'

'Someone typing deliberately slowly with one finger could purposefully create that effect.'

'Sounds like you don't need a typewriting expert; you seem to be pretty knowledgeable about these things.'

'Only because I recognise that kind of typing style as my own. This is what any pages I type come out looking like,' said Hugh. 'If only I had your Miss Williams to guide me with my technique.' He leaned back in his chair, thinking. 'Alice was the person who got you involved in all this, Bertie. It wouldn't be the first time someone has invited someone into a situation like this, in an attempt to convince the police of their innocence.'

'Yes, I was worried you might say something like that, too,' Bertie said, glumly.

The theatre manager strode back into the room carrying a bundle of papers with him. He seemed somewhat surprised to find two people in his office, but then he quickly remembered that they had also been there when he left. He sat down at the desk, rifled through the stack of papers and paused, looking up at the pair of them, who had been watching his every move. 'You don't need to take my fingerprints, do you? I'm a little busy for that sort of thing. I can tell you now, I don't think I've ever touched a typewriter in my life. Sorry, I know it doesn't seem appropriate for me to carry on working through all of this, but there is work to be done, refunds to be made.'

'Refunds? For the evening performance?' asked Bertie, with realisation.

'Of course.'

'Tell me, prior to that, the show was doing good business?'

'Oh yes, more than good enough. A play by Alice Crawford, that seemed to bring in the audiences alright. Not a sell-out, but not half bad by our current standards.'

'A husband-and-wife team in the lead roles too, that would have helped as well,' said Bertie.

Gareth looked off into the distance with a look of sadness. 'Poor Katherine,' he said, before returning his attention back to the ledgers on the desk, continuing his work while he talked. 'I think it was a good way of getting Anthony back onto the stage; he's fallen out of favour recently, although he was never a bad actor. It's not like they've fallen on hard times or anything, but I suppose he might have been taking it badly, being out of work.'

'Badly, in what way?'

'Well, we've all seen his mood change in recent weeks. Perhaps it's just because we're coming to the end of the run; it's always a bit of a tense time, especially if you don't have something lined up next.' Gareth shrugged. 'But you've seen what the pair of them were like; they were the perfect team, that's why they were perfect for this show. She would very much stand by her husband through anything, the bad times and the good. I feel for Katherine, it must be so hard losing someone who you were that close to, that committed to. All the administration to deal with, it's the last thing you need. She's here today, going through the things that she and Anthony left behind in their rooms.'

Gareth totalled up the final few figures in the ledger and then tossed the pencil aside. 'And so very close to making a profit...'

'How long can you keep things going without making any money?' asked Bertie.

'Not much longer, I have to say. We'll need another hit soon. But it gets so hard to persuade people to come here, you have to take anything. Once you get a reputation like that, it's very hard to break. We're a cursed venue.'

'Now, more than ever,' said Bertie, gravely.

Hugh, who had been sitting quietly in thought, interjected. 'Mr James, I want to ask you about people that hang about at the stage door.'

'Male admirers waiting at the stage door have a long tradition at the Gaiety. It doesn't surprise me.'

'Particularly a Mr Shilling?'

'Shilling.' Gareth sighed deeply. 'He's always hung around the theatres. Time was that he was a bit of a fixer, if you know what I'm saying. Could get his hands on things.'

Hugh leaned forward. 'What sort of things?'

'All sorts. You just asked him and he'd always be able to get his hands on it. If you needed a certain type of expensive fabric, in order to make a costume or some such, he'd be able to get it half the price. Tools, jewellery... All sorts.'

'And other, more nefarious, things?'

'Yes, he was able to get his hands on that sort of stuff too, I'm afraid,' the theatre manger admitted.

'Shilling was involved in gambling, wasn't he?' asked Bertie.

'Yes.' Gareth looked at them guiltily. 'How do you think I managed to place my own bet against the success of this show. It was Shilling who was able to make that sort of thing happen.'

Bertie sighed. 'So that was who Alice and I saw leave your office, wasn't it?'

Gareth nodded. 'I'm afraid you did.'

'He was around on the day of the matinee?' asked Bertie.

'No, not during the day, I would have known about it. People around here know him and it's not like he can

212

blend in easily. He's so tall and distinctive-looking.'

Hugh sat forward. 'But what about after the show? Could he have slipped in?'

Gareth looked at Bertie. 'Once you and Alice had left this office after the show, I went around the corridors just to check on things. I'm telling you, if I didn't see him, someone else would have.'

'Wait, you went around the dressing rooms?' asked Hugh.

Gareth nodded.

'But I thought said you were in your office with John Tay the whole time until Dennis found Mr Debenham?'

'Yes, I see what you mean. I suppose I must have left him for a short while, but he didn't move from this room.'

Hugh raised his eyebrows. 'As far as you know...'

'But what reason would he have to lie?' The theatre manager looked dumbfounded.

'Mr James, this is a murder. There might be every reason for him to lie,' said Hugh, gravely.

'But you can't possibly think...' Gareth was lost for words. 'They go back years, John and the Debenhams.'

'Yes.' Bertie nodded. 'But John and Katherine go back even further. There was once something between them years ago – he admitted it to Alice and me. That was before she and Anthony met; he was the one who introduced them to each other.'

Gareth shook his head. 'He's incredibly protective of her, he is of all his actors, but so much time has passed since then. Surely any feelings like that would have faded

213

long ago.'

'I don't know,' said Bertie, glancing at Hugh then back at the theatre manager. 'When it comes to things like love, the amount of time that has passed doesn't usually have any bearing on the matter.'

'Let's focus on Shilling for the time being,' said Hugh, changing the subject. 'Might he have had business with Anthony backstage? Perhaps there were drugs to be paid for, some other supplies or other debts to be settled?'

'I don't know that Anthony was into that sort of thing,' said Bertie. 'As we know, there might have been gambling debts, but the idea of anything else...'

'Anthony? There's no chance of that,' said Gareth, shaking his head. 'Shilling fell out of favour with the theatres. Here, along with many other places, wouldn't allow him anywhere near our backstage anymore, not once we realised he was going down that line of things.'

'But people still use him, for their personal needs?' asked Hugh. 'If I can put it like that?'

Gareth nodded. 'I'm afraid so. Not much we can do about things that take place outside the building. Actors getting up on stage every night and baring their souls for other people's personal enjoyment? I shouldn't like to wonder what their doctors prescribe them to send them off to sleep at night with all that adrenaline coursing through their bodies. For those that can't afford the doctor, there are people like Shilling who can get you what you need.'

A pang of guilt shot through Bertie. There were

always heightened emotions during his plays. Characters pushed to their limits, pushed to murder. Had he properly considered the toll it might be taking on the performers? It was just acting, wasn't it? Just pretending.

Bertie had stayed up late into the night with actors, still wide awake and exhilarated by the performance that had taken place. The difference was that once the play was up and running, he was able to return to his daily routine. For the actor, it was a toll that they continued to pay nightly.

'I don't condone it, I don't like it, and I certainly don't wish to see it on my watch. But it does happen,' said Gareth.

'Bertie!' Alice's booming voice interrupted them suddenly as she flew through the door in a rage. 'It's hard not to take this personally, you know. Being accused of murder now, am I?'

She looked around the room, at Hugh, the theatre manager and then back to Bertie. 'Well, what have you lot got to say for yourself?'

'I'm not accusing you of murder,' Bertie protested.

'Aren't you?'

'Well not exactly, no. I'm just saying that there is a possibility that you could have typed out the advert that was printed in the newspaper... Unlikely as that is, it is still a possibility, and all possibilities—'

'Yes, yes... They're all likely enough until they're unproven, or whatever it is you two like to say to each other,' Alice grumbled.

'But what is proven is that whoever typed it did so on your typewriter.'

'Well, I didn't type it, so you'll just have to take a leap of faith and believe me, I suppose.'

There was an awkward silence which Bertie was reluctant to fill with an answer, so he decided to ask another question. 'You had your typewriter at the theatre during rehearsals, I take it?'

'Of course. There are lots of changes to be made – as there always are. You know what it's like... I set up a little station in the front-of-house bar so I could clack away without disturbing anyone.'

'Who else knew that's where you had set up?' asked Hugh.

'Everyone, I suppose,' said Alice. 'It's not like it was a secret. Any of the people working at the theatre could have had access to it.'

'The advert was typed on Alice's typewriter, but the note that arrived on the day of the performance wasn't,' said Hugh, thinking aloud.

'Where is your typewriter now, Alice?' Bertie said coolly.

She narrowed her eyes. 'You know very well, Bertie, that it's on my desk at home. It's been there for ages, well before that advert was placed, you know. Weeks have passed. You don't suppose someone broke in to use it while I was out? That's a horrible thought...'

'I never saw a typewriter. I saw your desk and a

mountain of papers. I presumed it was buried underneath there, but—'

'Brilliant. He doesn't. He doesn't believe me,' Alice exclaimed.

'It's not that. It's a murder, Alice. We don't know who's involved. Anyone in this theatre could have done it. Including me.'

'Could you?' asked Hugh, with a clear note of surprise in his voice.

'Well, no. But it's the principle, isn't it,' said Bertie.

Alice nodded forcefully. 'Well as long as you all know that if it's possible for me to be a murderer, it's possible for Bertie here to be one, too,' she said, pointing an accusing finger at him.

Hugh smiled, commenting idly, 'Unless you're both in it together.'

They both shot a strikingly similar look in Hugh's direction.

He held his hands up in apology and stood up. 'Look, at least one person connected to this theatre is involved in this. You two are both connected.'

'Hugh,' Bertie said in protest, but Hugh held up a hand to silence him.

'I'm sorry, Bertie, Alice.' He addressed each one of them in turn. 'This was not a random killing. It was targeted, planned and in a devilishly clever way – which is why it seems impossible. Who better to come up with an impossible murder than two of Britain's leading playwrights?'

'Hugh, you can't be serious.'

'To be honest, Bertie, I am. I'm really not sure what to believe any more.'

Chapter Twenty-Two

22

Bertie felt guilty about leaving Alice behind after they'd just accused each other of being potential murderers, but with the revelation that Hugh wasn't quite as sure of his innocence as he first thought, Bertie felt he had no choice but to follow him out of the room.

They walked down the stairs and as they came to the corridor by Katherine Debenham's dressing room, they saw the door was open. As the two of them approached, Dennis left carrying two small cases stacked on top of each other. He disappeared down to the next floor and out of view.

'Yes, those can go to the car too, Elise,' came a voice from within. Moments later, Katherine's maid appeared at the door carrying a hat box. She noticed Hugh and Bertie and acknowledged them with a small nod, before following the same route downstairs that Dennis had taken.

Hugh stopped in the doorway, looking into the room. Katherine was sitting in a comfortable-looking armchair in the corner from where she had been directing proceedings from underneath a hat, which was large enough to shadow her face.

'Ah, Inspector,' she said, when she saw Hugh, inviting him in with an ambiguous but graceful wave of her hand. 'I'm afraid I've forgotten your name.'

'Inspector Chapman, Mrs Debenham. I hope you don't mind me popping by,' he said with a comforting smile. 'I've got Bertie out here too.'

'Of course, come in, both of you.'

As Hugh entered the room, Bertie took his place, hovering in the doorway.

Hugh inspected some of the items that were still yet to be packed away. 'You didn't have to come back here to take care of all of this. This could have all been done for you, you know.'

'Our things, mine and Tony's, they're all jumbled up together. I'd rather get things sorted out here at the theatre rather than send the lot back to our place and deal with them there. The thought of doing this all at home, what was our home... Well, it's rather overwhelming.' Emotion crept into her last few words and she stopped herself from saying any more.

'You didn't fancy using the bigger dressing room downstairs, the one next to the stage?' asked Hugh.

'The so-called "star" dressing room. We never liked to think of ourselves as stars, myself and Tony. We were just actors, the same as every other person in the company. The problem in taking the dressing room next to the stage is that it becomes a sort of informal green room. People end up endlessly popping in and out during the show. I much prefer the peace and quiet of having my own private space.'

'Your husband didn't mind moving up a floor?' Hugh said.

'Not at all. Besides, he thought it was better that the three girls should share that room instead. It was close to the stage – much more convenient for them and what the show required in terms of costume changes and so on.'

Katherine smiled, speaking slowly and deliberately, trying to keep the emotion from her voice. 'We were very much in love. I'm sure others have told you that. But spending all our time together at home as well as at the theatre, well, that may have been too much – at the same time, it doesn't seem enough. Although, as you said, he was nearby. Not too hard for him to get my attention whenever he needed to.' She smiled at the thought, but it slowly faded into sadness. 'If I'd known there was someone determined to...' She stopped to wipe a tear away that had appeared delicately at the corner of her eye. 'I don't know what I'm going to do without him.'

'I'm afraid I have a few more questions I need to ask you,' said Hugh.

Katherine nodded.

'Do you know anyone by the name of Harry Shilling?'

Katherine looked between Bertie and Hugh before answering. 'No, I can't say that I do.'

'You are aware that we found some fingerprints on your letter opener, which was used as the murder weapon, and that we could not identify them?'

'Yes.'

'We have now found that they match those found on a note which contained the text of the advert that was placed in the paper. We suspect they belong to a man named Harry Shilling.'

'Is that him? Is he the man who killed my Tony?'

Hugh held up his hand to gently stop her from saying any more. 'You've never seen him at the stage door? Perhaps as a well-wisher? We found a picture of you and your husband outside the theatre that had been drawn by him.'

'I don't ever recall someone sketching me. Perhaps he did the drawings from memory. I meet any number of people at the stage door. It's not unknown for someone in my position to have fans.' She looked at Bertie. 'You know what it's like.'

Bertie smiled. 'Luckily, I manage to escape the worst of it. Actors' faces are well known, a playwright's is less so.'

'Well, I suppose it's alright for you.' She looked slightly put out, then puzzled. 'But I don't understand. If this Shilling did it, how did he get past the stage door? Someone would have seen him.'

'That's what we're trying to ascertain,' said Hugh. 'My fellow officers are looking into it, but so far we have no eyewitness accounts of anyone seeing him in the building. Mr James is insistent that he wouldn't be able to get inside without being recognised.'

'I don't understand why he would want to kill Tony.'

'Jealousy,' Bertie offered. 'Could he have been obsessed with you? Perhaps a certain type of person with a delusion of some sort?'

'I hardly think that's likely.'

'There is one other alternative,' said Hugh gravely. 'When we found Mr Debenham's body, we know that the curtains were drawn and the lights were off. And it was *your* dressing room, Mrs Debenham.'

'At the time of the murder, the room may have not been well lit...' Bertie took a cautious step forward, as he thought through the scenario for himself.

Katherine put up a hand to interrupt him. 'Do you mean to say that perhaps this man was trying to kill me?'

'It's a possibility we have to entertain,' said Hugh. 'There was no contact, no altercation, perhaps a stage door where you gave him the brush off?'

'I am always generous with my fans after the show. I assure you if there was any animosity held by this man, it was not instigated by me.'

'Talking of altercations, had there been any disagreements between you and your husband recently?'

'Absolutely not.'

'It's just that we have heard that there was an

exchange between the two of you regarding a missing sum of money.'

'And who told you that, may I ask?' she said, brusquely.

'I'm afraid I'm not at liberty—'

'Oh tosh,' Katherine interrupted. 'I know very well who it was, that damned chauffeur.'

'So, it's true?' asked Bertie.

'The chauffeur didn't make it up if that's what you mean. No, I'm sure he was very accurate in his retelling of it.'

She stopped for a moment, repositioning herself in the chair. Hugh purposefully stayed silent, waiting for her to fill the silence.

'Yes, money had gone missing,' she said. 'Naturally I assumed that Anthony was up to his old habits again.'

'And you know that it was him taking the money?' asked Hugh.

'Well, who else could it be?'

'Perhaps we should take a visit to your bank. Where do you bank, Mrs Debenham?'

'Oh, that won't help you,' she replied with a dismissive wave of her hand. 'The money wasn't withdrawn from our bank; it was taken from our safe at the house.'

'I see,' said Hugh. 'And only you and Mr Debenham had the key or combination for it?'

'Combination. Yes, that's right. You see, that's why I know it couldn't have been someone else. I didn't say anything at first. I thought, perhaps, that the whole thing would just burn itself out. Especially since he was about to be back in work again.'

'But it didn't stop. You had to confront him in the end,' said Bertie.

'That's right. We were good for the money – well, only as long as the habit didn't continue for an eternity. I noticed that the money kept being taken and eventually I decided to confront him about it.'

'What did he have to say about that?' asked Hugh.

'As our reliable driver will have undoubtedly told you, he denied it.'

'And you had no reason to suspect anyone else?'

'None. Besides, after I confronted him about the business, the money stopped disappearing. I'd say that's pretty conclusive.'

Bertie leaned against the countertop, which formed the dressing table. 'You never confirmed where the money was going, what it was for.' It was more like a statement than a question.

'No,' Katherine replied. A note of unease had crept into her voice.

'The assumption, naturally, was that he'd settled back into his old ways: gambling. But there could have been other reasons, other debts. Another woman, blackmail even?'

Katherine's expression hardened and she spoke pointedly. 'I would remind you, Bertie, that my dear husband has only recently been taken from me. That kind of speculation is as wild as it is offensive. The idea is ridiculous.'

'But we're talking of Anthony returning to old ways; it's not out of the question.'

'That affair was a malicious rumour,' she said, barely able to hide her anger now.

'No, it wasn't,' said Bertie, quietly.

Hugh put a hand on Bertie's shoulder, encouraging him to stop, but it was already too late.

Katherine rose sharply from her seat. 'I think we're done here,' she said forcefully.

'Is everything alright, ma'am?' asked Elise, who had just returned to the dressing room.

'It's fine, dear. Mr Carroll and the inspector were just on their way out.'

'Thank you, Mrs Debenham,' Hugh said, in the most professional tone he could muster. 'We may need to speak to you again.'

'I'm sure you will,' Katherine replied as she pointed to the open door.

Elise stood aside and ushered the two of them out into the corridor.

When the door had closed behind them and they had moved a little further along the corridor, Hugh stopped and turned. 'Bertie,' he said in a warning tone, 'you can't get carried away like that.'

It was like being told off by a schoolmaster; Bertie felt he had let Hugh down. 'That reaction, though, Hugh. She did know.' He spoke enthusiastically but faltered when he saw the expression on his friend's face. 'I'm sorry.'

'I know, just... Maybe let me do the questions from now on.'

'Deal,' Bertie agreed. 'However, there's something about her maid just now. She looks familiar.'

'Well, I'm sure she's been around theatrical circles as long as her employer has,' said Hugh.

'No, from somewhere else.'

The dressing room door clicked open and Elise emerged with another box of belongings to be taken down to the car. She gave them a stern look as she went past, in the protective way that only a maid can.

'You're a singer,' Bertie said, as it suddenly came to him. Elise stopped in her tracks. 'At Betty's. I saw you there the other night, with Alice.'

She turned slowly to face them both. 'I'm sorry, sir. You must have me confused with someone else.'

'No, I don't. I didn't recognise you at first because of your uniform.'

'What if I am?' Elise asked. 'Doesn't have anything to do with you, does it? Doesn't have anything to do with no murders either, does it?'

'No, I suppose not,' said Bertie, a little humbled.

'Does Mrs Debenham know?' asked Hugh.

'Know that I'm being held up from doing my work by you two? No, she doesn't, but *I'll* certainly know about it if you don't let me get on.'

'About the singing?' Hugh clarified, pushing for an answer.

'No, she doesn't. But I don't know that it makes much difference whether she does or not, it doesn't affect my work and I only ever do it when it's my night off.'

'They don't notice you coming back in the early hours of the morning?' asked Bertie.

'It's a theatrical household. After a performance, Mr and Mrs Debenham are often up themselves until the early hours. You try getting to sleep after a show like this one with adrenaline still coursing through your veins.'

Hugh nodded. 'Did Mr or Mrs Debenham ever take a sleeping draught?'

'Sometimes,' she said, thinking carefully. 'It would have been only on the rare occasion. However, there were times when they might need to take something to help send them off to sleep.'

'Any idea what it was?' asked Hugh. Bertie noticed that his friend's notebook was open, ready for scribbling in.

'Whatever it was the doctor prescribed, I suppose. Veranol or something else of the sort.' She glanced nervously at the dressing room door.

'Are you not worried, travelling back late at night or even during the early hours of the morning?'

'I can look after myself, you know. If Arthur can slip away with the car, sometimes he'll be waiting to take me back.'

'You two are close, then?' asked Bertie.

'Nothing inappropriate, if that's what you're suggesting.' She narrowed her eyes at him. 'Now, if you don't mind, I must really be on my way.'

Hugh nodded and put the notebook back in his pocket; the maid shot off down the corridor hoping to make up lost time.

'I suppose you mean one of *your* bars, Bertie,' said Hugh, turning to face him with a disapproving look and a raised eyebrow.

'Betty's isn't that bad,' said Bertie with a smile. 'It's down on Greek Street, under—'

Hugh quickly interrupted him. 'I don't need to know.'

Bertie laughed. 'Oh, come on. It's only a bar.' He opened his mouth, ready to continue talking, but Hugh silenced him with a look.

'I'm serious. I'm a police officer and you're—'

'Yes?' interrupted Bertie, anticipating the next word.

'Not.' Hugh looked at him with a serious expression. 'It's not that simple. It's not just that I don't want to know about these things. I *can't* know about them. Do you understand? I might be under obligation to report it.'

Despite their physical closeness in the cramped corridor and even though they shared the same streets in the self-same city, Bertie was suddenly aware that their worlds had never felt further apart. 'Report what, Hugh? It's just dancing.'

'Well, it bloody well better be,' said Hugh, grumpily, as he set off down the corridor, leaving Bertie standing there by himself. This time Bertie's legs felt too heavy to chase after him.

Chapter Twenty-Three

As he emerged out of the stage door and onto the familiar curve of Aldwych, Bertie was feeling a little lost. He couldn't quite find his footing and wasn't quite sure what he should do. Should he hang around and see if Hugh showed up again, or should he just head off home?

The thought of doing any more investigating by himself didn't seem to be an option, not while there was no one to do it with. He seemed to have lost Hugh and he wasn't convinced that Alice would want to spend any time with him at the moment either. Besides, he wasn't sure what more there was to learn. Apart from the elusive Harry Shilling, they had spoken to everyone he could think of who might have been connected with the murder.

Parked alongside the theatre was the Debenhams' sleek silver car. Elise was placing the belongings from the dressing room neatly into the boot. Arthur, with a cigarette tucked behind his ear, helped with some of the more awkward items. He saw Bertie standing there and gave him a friendly wave. Elise seemed less impressed and avoided looking at him until she disappeared back inside.

Arthur approached Bertie, lighting his cigarette as his did so. 'Mr Carroll. It's been a long time since I've had the pleasure of driving for you.'

'It has,' he replied, smiling. 'You must have driven for all of us at some point over the years, before you went to work for the Debenhams. Me, Alice, John?'

Arthur nodded. 'Of course, Alice was always good for a bit of gossip, I seem to remember.'

'Yes, I bet she was,' said Bertie, with a note of disapproval in his voice.

'Are you leaving as well?'

Bertie nodded.

'This inspector friend of yours. You're sure that he'll be able get to the bottom of this?'

'Of course,' Bertie replied.

'Good.' Arthur smiled. 'That's good.'

'You were close to Mr Debenham?'

'As close as any man is to his employer, I suppose. I certainly want to see his murderer be brought to justice. I think we all do.'

'You were witness to the conversation about the missing money,' said Bertie, conspiratorially. 'What do you make of it? Is it likely that Anthony would have fallen back into his bad habits?'

Arthur shook his head. 'I couldn't say. I don't get to see what goes on behind the closed doors of these clubs. You can tell if someone's having a good day or a bad day, but you usually don't get to know why and it's inappropriate to ask.'

'Of course,' said Bertie. 'But would you say that he was having more bad days than good recently?'

'The news that he was going to be back on stage, that was good. You could see that he was energised again. Performing on stage is what an actor lives for, isn't it? But you understand, it's not like Mr Debenham was in the depths of a depression before this work came along.'

'No?'

'Not at all, if anything...' Arthur tailed off.

Bertie leaned closer. 'Go on.'

'Well, he couldn't have been in better spirits for most of the run. Everyone saw there was a change in him in the last few days. I'm not sure if it was because it was coming to a close, but everything became a little more serious with him. Things weren't as light as they had been at the start, if that makes sense.'

'I think it does. When that advert first appeared, I think everyone was affected by it in some way or another. Some people took it more seriously than others, I suppose.'

'Well, yes, but that's the funny thing. Mr Debenham didn't take the advert all that seriously. He thought it was just someone playing a joke; it was Mrs Debenham who seemed more worried about it.'

'She seemed pretty confident about continuing with

the show on the day. Alice and I saw her speaking to the rest of the cast. John seemed the wariest of going ahead, but I suppose directors are quite protective of their actors.'

'She might have come round to the idea, perhaps Mr Debenham had persuaded her. While he wasn't worried about the advert, he was worried about *something*. I'm sure that started before the advert was printed.'

Bertie thought for a moment, processing this change in Anthony Debenham's mood and wondering what could have caused it.

'Elise mentioned it to me as well. It's only memorable because it's very rare to find a closed door in the Debenhams' household. She told me that one day she had been upstairs and the door to Mr Debenham's office was closed. He'd been making some phone calls, which sounded very serious by the tone of his voice, but she couldn't make out what he was saying. She'll kill me for mentioning this, she doesn't think it's proper and correct for us to talk about our employers this way.'

'These calls he was making, they were after Mrs Debenham had noticed the money had gone missing?'

Arthur smiled, relieved. 'Of course, it must have been that...'

'It doesn't seem that a gambling habit was entirely out of the question then?'

'Maybe not, but something's a bit odd about the whole thing.'

'What's that?' asked Bertie.

'I know we all have our own sins to hide, but to steal from your own safe... It doesn't make sense. Does that sound like something Mr Debenham would do?'

'I'm not sure I could say what he would do any more,' said Bertie. 'Sometimes it's best to put our own assumptions aside when it comes to these things.'

'I know Mrs Debenham kept a tight rein on the finances and anything unaccounted for would have been discovered in time. But removing cash from the safe is a sure-fire way of getting yourself noticed.'

Bertie nodded. 'That's true, unless he had no other option. If he needed the money quickly, it was right there to hand.' He paused. 'And the question of an affair?'

Arthur laughed. 'No question at all. Me and Elise have only been working for the Debenhams these last few years, there's been no hint of something like that happening while we've been there. In the past, perhaps... I wouldn't know either way.'

'Why are you so sure?'

'How would Mr Debenham have an affair without me knowing? I drive him everywhere.'

'Of course,' Bertie chuckled.

'Talking of driving, I would offer you a lift but, once we're loaded up with all these things from the dressing rooms, there might not even be room for me.'

'That's alright,' said Bertie. 'I'm not really on your way.'

'Plenty of taxis around,' Arthur said, offering some hint of consolation.

'I think I'll get the tube – Holborn. It's cooler down there, at least.'

'Right you are, Mr Carroll,' he said with a professional nod.

Bertie wandered away from the stage door, the thoughts of the murder still buzzing in his head. After walking a short distance along the pavement, he turned back to the theatre, wondering whether he should hang around or wait for Hugh or Alice.

Before he could scan around for any sign of him, Bertie's eyes were drawn back to Elise and Arthur. She had just returned, emerging from the theatre with more belongings to be packed into the car. Both seemed deep in conversation for a few moments, then Elise glanced in Bertie's direction. He smiled, giving them both a wave which wasn't returned.

Clearly, she was still annoyed at him, although Bertie thought nothing of it as he turned, leaving Aldwych behind and heading in the direction of Holborn Underground station.

He appreciated the walk. Often it was easier to think on your feet, and plenty of shoe leather had been worn through while Bertie was writing his plays. Friends in the theatre community were used to seeing him pace the streets of the West End, and his neighbours were used to the sight of him doing laps of the block where he lived in Belsize Park. The other occupants of the apartments were often less happy to be disturbed by his secretary, who would be forced to call out from his third-floor window to remind him that he was due at an important appointment. He could become so absorbed in his own thoughts that it might take several attempts to get his attention. There had only been one occasion, when he was so deep in thought, that she had resorted to throwing scrunched up balls of newspaper at him.

Bertie was shaken out of his thoughts by a rattling tram as it emerged from its subterranean journey underneath Kingsway. There was also something else emerging in his mind, but he couldn't quite latch on to the full idea yet.

He shook away the idea of solving the crime and let his thoughts drift back to Hugh. As each moment passed, his friend's comments seemed to cut a little deeper. At the same time, he began to feel frustration rather than anger towards him.

Of course, Bertie understood that Hugh might not be able to actively participate in the sort of social life he had, but to try to suppress all mention of it? Perhaps Hugh was right – it wasn't personal. Perhaps it really was because he didn't want to know, as he would have felt an obligation to report anything. Hugh was professional to a fault.

That was where the frustration lay, the fact that he seemingly couldn't separate his work life from his personal one. The thought caused Bertie to give a wry chuckle to himself. Who was he to comment on the line between personal and professional? In the world of theatre, there often wasn't one. In the world of the police detective, there had to be.

Absorbed in his thoughts, Bertie disappeared into the yawning entrance of Holborn Station, descending the long escalators down to the platform.

He found that the mechanical vibrations whirling away underneath his feet had the same effect as wandering the streets. In fact, he enjoyed luxuriating in the stillness, allowing his thoughts to occupy him, as people hurried down the steps beside him.

It was approaching the end-of-day rush and as Bertie arrived on the platform, it was already full of bodies awkwardly trying to shuffle their way along.

Because the hours of the theatrical trade were often not in synchronisation with the wider working world, Bertie could usually avoid the busy times on public transport. He wondered whether choosing the Underground had been an error in judgement. As he was jostled along by the crowd, the station began to feel a little airless. He could feel the air begin to rush into the station as the train approached, as if responding to Bertie's thoughts.

What began as a gentle breeze grew to a more forceful gust of air. Bertie could feel it ruffling his hair as he manoeuvred himself closer to the edge of the platform. Then came a different feeling, altogether more physical. The bodies around him seemed to brace and tense, but it wasn't enough. A small surge of movement from behind pushed him forward.

He reached out for something to grab on to, but in front of him there was nothing but air. He found himself falling down onto the track, helpless.

To his immediate left there was a scream. Another passenger – a woman – had been caught up in the movement and toppled down onto the track with him.

Everything seemed to lose focus for a moment. There were people shouting, but he couldn't understand what they were saying. People further down the platform were moving their arms in a blur, trying to attract the attention of the train driver, who was still a little way off in the darkened tunnel.

Thankfully Bertie seemed to have not lost his footing altogether and managed to scramble back to his feet, the right side of his body aching with pain in the various places that he had landed. He quickly reached a hand out, helping the woman to her feet. With the assistance of some of the other passengers up on the platform they managed to unceremoniously bundle her back to safety.

Then he turned and saw it. He froze.

The flat red front of the underground train had burst from the tunnel at the far end of the platform and was hurtling towards him. Bertie could only concentrate on one thing, his own voice shouting inside his head.

Move!

But his voice seemed to have no effect, his muscles refused to budge on command. Hands grappled hopelessly at his shoulders, in an attempt to manoeuvre him and drag him to safety.

The loud screech of brakes was deafening, filling the station with noise.

'Bertie!' came a shout, that somehow penetrated the chaos. Suddenly everything snapped back into focus.

He turned to his left to find an outstretched hand reaching out for him. Bertie threw his own hand into it and a strong arm lifted him, half dragged him, up from the track. The two of them found themselves lying together on the cold hard floor of the platform. His rescuer held him tightly, keeping him safely in place and shielding him from the large metal carriages which whizzed past them, finally coming to a stop.

While his body had begun to work again, his brain seemed to remain frozen. Bertie couldn't quite work out what had happened. He already knew, by some kind of instinct, who his rescuer was.

'Hugh?'

Bertie held on tightly to him, while dozens of relieved and enquiring eyes peered down on them. He didn't want to let go.

There was nothing Hugh could do except let out a thankful laugh, which caused Bertie to do the same. The relief was overwhelming, exhilarating even. It seemed inappropriate in the circumstances, but neither of them cared. They continued laughing as the other concerned passengers watched on.

Chapter Twenty-Four

24

The smartly dressed London Underground employees had tried to sort things out the best they could, but as no one had seen anything suspicious or noticed anyone who could have caused the incident, everyone was sent on their way.

Thankfully, Bertie had sustained no injuries other than a few bruises and grazes. The young woman who had fallen to the track with him was in a similar condition, but was understandably shaken.

That hadn't stopped Hugh from fussing over him as they made their way home in a hastily summoned police car.

'You're a highly trained detective, Hugh. I can't believe you didn't see anything,' Bertie exclaimed.

'It was a crowded platform.'

'But you didn't recognise anyone on your way over from the theatre? Someone was either following me or they were following you.'

Hugh shifted uncomfortably. 'I'm afraid I had something of a one-track mind and wasn't really paying attention to much else.'

'Right.'

'I wanted to apologise. I'm afraid I might have lost my temper, a little, and I shouldn't have.'

Bertie sighed, but then an idea occurred to him. 'How did you know I was headed that way? I could have gone anywhere after I left the theatre.'

'The driver, he knew. He said you'd just left and pointed me in the right direction.'

'Where was Elise?'

'Inside, I presume,' said Hugh.

'But you didn't actually see her. What if she was already on her way to try and kill me?'

'The maid, Bertie? I think that's stretching things a little.'

'Someone did. Someone's murdered one person already, why not one more?'

'Or it could simply have been an accident.'

Bertie didn't seem satisfied by that particular solution but broke out in a broad smile.

'What is it?' asked Hugh, noticing his expression.

'You came to apologise to me and ended up saving my life.'

'Yes, that was rather good of me, wasn't it? You saved

the life of that woman too, Bertie. You're a hero.'

'Thank you,' said Bertie, solemnly.

'It still doesn't change things. While I'm still a police officer, I couldn't bear the idea of you thinking that I might not like you, personally. And perhaps you might hate me for it.'

Bertie gave a light chuckle. 'I can promise you, Hugh, I could never hate you for anything.'

'Good,' Hugh said with satisfaction. 'Well, I feel the same way entirely.'

Bertie frowned, returning his thoughts to the murder. 'It does put a spanner in the works though.'

'It does?'

'Of our theory. If there was someone backstage, among the crowd, they might not be recognised at all. I know, when it came to this incident, we were both distracted in our own ways, but if there *was* someone at the tube station from the theatre, neither of us saw them. Perhaps whoever it was could have slipped by unnoticed backstage after all.'

Hugh nodded. 'Something doesn't add up. I can't see what yet, but there's still a piece of this puzzle missing. Anthony's guests...'

'The one he turned away on the day?'

'Any of them, really. The unfriendly-looking faces – that's how the stage door keeper put it. And there's this change in his mood. I think the timing of it must mean something.'

'I thought that, too,' said Bertie. 'At first I thought it

might be to do with before or after the advert was placed, but that doesn't line up correctly.'

'No, it doesn't,' Hugh agreed.

'I think his mood changed when it was discovered that money was going missing from the safe.'

'It makes sense; if the reason Anthony had taken the money from the safe was to pay off a debt, he wouldn't have been too happy about it.'

'Or perhaps there's something else going on there. There is something in the timing of this whole thing that we're missing.'

Before he could elaborate further, the police car pulled up outside the familiar red brick block of flats where Bertie lived. The two of them clambered out of the vehicle. In front of them, a short footpath led up to the entrance where the door was held ajar. Waiting in the doorway, with a worried expression on her face, was Bertie's secretary. Even with her deeply concerned look, the sight of her never failed to bring a smile to his face.

'Gertie,' Bertie said as he approached. 'Am I glad to see you!'

'Well, Mr Carroll, I sure am glad to see you too, although I've been sick with worry. Ever since you got yourself mixed up in another murder, I knew something like this would happen. Why you can't just stay here and write plays rather than go off gallivanting around the West End, I don't know. No offence, Inspector,' she finished with a nod at Hugh.

'I can't stay inside all the time,' Bertie jokingly

protested.

'Oh yes, you can! I'm going to make absolutely sure of it. I've a right mind to clip you around the ear for the stress you've caused me.' As her voice started to raise in volume, so did the strength of her Trinidadian accent.

'So much for being safer at home,' commented Bertie.

Gertie held the inner door open, guiding them into the hallway. 'I made sure the lift is here, so we can take you up.'

'Really, there's no need. I can walk perfectly fine. I can manage the stairs.'

She ignored Bertie, looking at Hugh for confirmation instead. 'Is that true, Inspector Chapman?'

'No damage has been done, Miss Williams, just a few bruises.'

'I think we'll take the lift, just to be sure, you know.'

'Okay,' replied Bertie. 'I should have learned by now never to disagree with you.'

'Yes, you certainly should have,' she replied with a smile, leading the three of them into the lift.

Hugh shut the lattice gates behind them and they began their ascent upwards. Bertie counted the floors as they went past.

When they reached the third, the efficient secretary led them all into Bertie's flat, where the door was already waiting open.

'Take a seat, Mr Carroll,' said Gertie, ushering him into a chair.

Bertie opened his mouth to protest that he didn't need

any special treatment, then closed it again. He knew there was no point arguing.

'Now, is there anything you need?' she asked.

Bertie sat comfortably in one of the armchairs next to his desk. 'Yes, actually. Can you dig up some information on one of Alice's shows?'

She raised her eyebrows, giving him a look that a mother would give a misbehaving child. 'I meant, would you like a cup of tea? I've got a pot brewed, just in case. Inspector, would you mind bringing it through?'

Hugh nodded his head. He disappeared through the small door that led to the kitchen and returned a few moments later with a tray that had been neatly laid out with tea things.

While he did so, Gertie admonished him sarcastically. 'Could I look into something for you?' she repeated with an unimpressed look. 'You're supposed to be resting, not thinking.'

'I assure you, I'm perfectly well. I'm sat here in this chair, being waited on by both of you. It's just a little detail I want to check. It can't do any harm.'

Hugh left her carefully thinking about it, while he poured out the tea into three cups on the edge of Bertie's immaculately clean desk.

'Fine,' Gertie snapped. 'I have considered your request and I will go through there and look up the required information, but you have to promise me that you won't move from that chair.'

'I wouldn't dare,' said Bertie with a smile. 'It was a

couple of years ago, maybe three or four. One of Alice's plays involving fingerprints.'

'Yes, I remember that,' she replied instantly, and disappeared into her small study. She returned almost immediately having pulled four bound volumes from one of the bookcases.

Putting them all on Bertie's desk she picked up the topmost one and began scanning the table of contents. After only a short few moments, the book was placed down on the desk and it was the turn of the next volume in the pile.

As she moved on to the third and then, finally, the fourth, an idea suddenly hit Bertie. His hand was hovering, raised in the air, as if he was trying to grab on to the thought before it vanished again.

'They're all the same!' he exclaimed, to a bemused Gertie and Hugh.

First the confused secretary looked at the pile of books and then she turned to Bertie. 'Of course they're all the same. The bookbinder makes sure of it. He tried to use a book cloth that was half a shade lighter once, but I can promise you he won't be making that mistake again in a hurry.'

'But I mean they're *exactly* the same.'

Gertie rolled her eyes, a little overdramatically. 'Are you sure you didn't do any damage when hit your head Mr Carroll?'

Bertie spoke slowly to Hugh, who had turned to look at the bound volumes. 'Those books, one on top of the other. They're all the same.'

Gertie looked down at the stack on the desk, gently resting her hand on top of them, protectively.

'We've got to get back to the theatre!' Bertie exclaimed, attempting to climb back out of the chair.

'Mr Carroll,' Gertie said sternly, making Bertie think twice about getting up. 'This is exactly what I was talking about. Don't you dare move a muscle.' She pointed a finger at him in warning.

Bertie smiled. 'We have to.' He turned to Hugh. 'I think I've just worked out how Anthony Debenham could have been murdered. It's like we said in the car, something to do with the timing. It's all thanks to you, Gertie. You're a genius.'

'Well, yes, I know I am a genius,' she said, without a hint of irony. 'But I don't see what that has to do with anything.'

'Do you understand what I mean, Hugh?'

Hugh nodded and broke into a large smile. 'I think I know exactly how Anthony Debenham was killed too.'

'Let me explain it to you both and if you think I'm right, then Gertie, you've got to let me and Hugh go back.'

'You can't go back to the theatre, they'll be in the middle of fitting up their next show,' said Gertie.

Bertie thought for a moment. 'Well, how about Romano's instead? In fact, I think Romano's would be the perfect location to solve this murder.'

'Well, you're not going anywhere without me. Especially as you're about to tell me, in detail, exactly how I solved it.' Gertie placed the final volume on top of the other and tapped a finger lightly on the stack of books. 'Also, you'll never guess who was in that play.' She smiled in Bertie's direction.

'I bet you I can,' said Hugh. 'And I suspect they own a typewriter that we'd be very interested in taking a look at.'

Bertie looked at Hugh. 'You know, I was just about to say the same thing.'

Chapter Twenty-Five

25

It took several hours for everyone to finally gather downstairs in the American Bar at Romano's, which would remain quiet and empty until later in the night. In the restaurant upstairs, the pre-theatre rush was running out of steam and coming to an end. Alice had been first to arrive, carrying her typewriter in its travel case. Tentatively, she approached Hugh and Bertie, who were hovering near one of the booths at the edge of the room. She deposited the machine on the table with a thunk.

'I'm taking this on trust, Bertie,' she said, nodding towards the valuable piece of evidence she had brought with her. 'I hope you know what you're doing.'

'We do,' said Bertie, although he couldn't quite force a smile.

She turned without a word and made her way to one

of the small tables in the centre of the room, where she sat patiently, waiting for the proceedings to begin. As time wore on, the rest of the tables were slowly filled as people arrived and edged their way into their seats.

Danny Owen looked particularly sullen as he wandered into the room, doing his best to avoid everyone's gaze. John Tay and Gareth James had decided to share a table together, although they both sat there in a stony silence. Margo arrived soon after but elected not to take a seat at any of the tables. Instead, she loitered at the side near the back, standing with her arms folded.

Bertie's stomach turned. He wondered if Hugh was feeling the same way, like two performers nervous in the moments before the curtain was due to rise. When Katherine Debenham arrived, there was no doubt that they were in a place of performance. She strode in, not forcefully, but with a purpose. It was almost as if she was making an entrance in her own play. Whatever the circumstances, she had unwittingly become the tragic star of this show. Elise and Arthur entered closely behind, her supporting players, following loyally.

She took a seat at the empty table that was closest to Bertie and Hugh, sitting elegantly across the room from Danny Owen. Even though everyone's eyes were inevitably drawn to the star performer, no one wanted to acknowledge each other. Instead, they avoided looking at anyone, preferring to pretend that no one else was there.

Hugh cleared his throat. 'Now we're all assembled, let's begin.' He spoke with a quiet voice, but with a calm confidence that meant he could be clearly heard by everyone who was gathered there.

There was a slight disturbance at the back of the room, causing everyone to turn. 'Not quite everyone,' came a youthful voice. Dennis appeared, standing next to a police constable who was stationed at the entrance to the restaurant. He was holding Dennis back, preventing him from entering. 'You're not starting without me, are you?'

The constable looked at Hugh, asking permission as to whether he should let the call boy past. Hugh nodded and Dennis trotted forward with a grin.

'After all, I was the one who discovered the body. I ought to be here to find out who it was that done him in.'

Katherine emitted a startled noise, causing Bertie to hold up a hand in apology.

'Maybe it's best if you sit over here with my secretary,' Bertie said hurriedly, in a hushed voice, diverting Dennis quickly towards Gertie, who sat in one of the booths at the side of the room. She shuffled along the seat so she could make room for him and Dennis gleefully hopped up next to her. If you hadn't known better, you might think that he was settling in for a night in at the movies.

Bertie looked back to Hugh and nodded.

'Let's begin again, then,' said Hugh, with a wry smile. 'On Wednesday an advert was placed in *The Era* which advertised a murder that was apparently going to take place during the Saturday matinee performance of Alice Crawford's play.'

Alice shuffled awkwardly in her seat at the mention of her own name. At the same time, Bertie carried her typewriter and put it on a small round table next to Hugh, so that everyone could get a good view of it.

From his inside pocket, Hugh retrieved the note which had the text of the advert on it and placed it down on the table next to Alice's typewriter.

'The text of the advert was typed on this machine, owned by the playwright herself.'

Across the room heads turned and spectators craned their necks as they tried to get a better view of Alice, who now looked more uncomfortable than ever.

'These exact words were copied out by Harry Shilling when he visited *The Era* office to place the advert. Each word was copied out by hand, carefully, making sure it matched the text he had been given by someone in this room.'

Hugh scanned the room to see if those words had any effect, but his audience were impassive.

'One wonders if he had instructions to destroy that note once he had completed the job he was hired to do, but he didn't. So, that can only mean that Alice is the mastermind behind this scheme.'

'Certainly not,' Alice objected, indignant at the suggestion.

'But this typewriter has been in your possession this whole time, hasn't it? It was at the theatre for a while, during rehearsals, but it's been at your home during the entire run of the show.'

'Long enough for it to be buried under that mountain of paperwork I saw the other morning,' said Bertie.

'That's quite true,' said Alice. 'I haven't typed on it for weeks, even though I really should have been making progress on my next play. You know how it is... I can say, quite certainly, that I haven't been typing any threatening advertisements.'

'But it was definitely typed on your typewriter,' Hugh said. 'And that advert was only placed last week. That fact is not in doubt. The advert was treated by most as a practical joke and not taken seriously, until a second anonymous note showed up on the morning of the matinee performance.'

Hugh retrieved the second note from his jacket and placed it on the table. 'This note, however, was *not* typed on this typewriter. That's rather unusual, wouldn't you say? Why the change in equipment?'

Bertie nodded. 'The problem was that the advert wasn't being taken seriously enough. It was only when this note arrived that everyone started to become worried. That's when Alice decided to call me.'

'That's exactly the reason why the anonymous note had to be sent – to bring more people to the theatre. But whoever wrote this note chose to use a different typewriter. For what reason and whose typewriter did they use?' asked Hugh.

He looked to the back of the room and nodded to one of the guarding constables at the door. Weaving through the tables, the man brought a travel case that presumably contained a second typewriter. Reaching the front, he placed it on the table behind the second note, which lay there guiltily.

'Perhaps this typewriter?' Hugh said as he unclipped the travel case and removed the lid, revealing the typewriter inside. 'Miss Williams, would you mind?'

Gertie slid out from the booth where she was sat with Dennis and walked over. Even though she was slightly nervous about being the centre of attention, she didn't show it as she pulled a chair up in front of the second typewriter. Hugh handed her a sheet of blank paper, which she loaded into the machine in a swift, professional manner.

With both eyes fixed on the note, which still lay on the table, she began copy-typing it expertly. The hammers moved in a percussive blur as they produced words on the paper.

Hugh cleared his throat, getting the typist's attention. 'Sorry, Miss Williams, could you do it worse?'

'Hmm.' Gertie sounded rather unimpressed. 'Yes, Mr Chapman, if that's what you'd like me to do. I suppose I could bear it for a few moments.'

'Please,' he replied, smiling.

Gertie hammered each key down, one at a time, using only her index fingers to navigate the keyboard. Each press of the keys looked like it was personally wounding the secretary, who was immensely proud of her typing skills. However, the purposefully bad technique was having the right effect. Now when the letters appeared on the sheet of paper, each one was printed once, then as the hammer bounced back onto the page, a second time – each letter double-printing, exactly as it had done in the original note.

Once she had finished her work, she pulled the sheet out of the top of the typewriter and handed it to Hugh. She then quickly departed back to her booth, sitting back down next to Dennis, as if she didn't want to stay and be associated with such shoddy workmanship.

Hugh inspected the two different notes carefully to see what similarities there were between the two. He held them up to his audience. 'Identical, I'd say. Wouldn't you?'

Hugh turned, showing the two pieces of paper up to Bertie, who nodded.

'Well, this is all very entertaining I'm sure,' came a voice from the back of the room. Margo was standing there with her arms folded. She looked on impatiently. 'Whose typewriter is that?'

'Constable?' said Hugh, addressing the policeman who had brought it in earlier.

'We retrieved this typewriter earlier today from Mr Owen's flat.'

As soon as Danny Owen's name was mentioned, every single person in the room snapped their head in his direction. Katherine Debenham shot him a look that could only be described as pure loathing. Danny sat still, seeming to be focusing very hard on the tabletop, not wanting to look up.

'Mr Owen, do you deny that this is your typewriter?' Hugh asked.

He braved a glance at Hugh. 'I don't deny that it is a typewriter from my flat, no.' He folded his arms defensively and leaned back in his chair. 'Although that's probably more typing on it than I've ever done.'

'I thought you said you were writing a book or even a play?' asked Bertie.

'*Thinking* about writing a book or a play I think you'll find, if you were listening properly.' Danny shook his head and shrugged. 'I couldn't think of a damn thing to write about, if I'm being honest.'

'Not as easy as is looks, is it?' commented Alice from the other side of the room with a wry chuckle. 'Go on then, Bertie. Who could have used that typewriter?'

'Why not you, Alice?'

The smile fell from her face. 'Well, thank you very much, Bertie. You told me I could trust you both. I thought you were working on some clever way to prove my innocence, not stab me in the back and accuse me instead.'

'But why not, Miss Crawford?' said Hugh, sounding serious. 'Your typewriter hasn't been at the theatre for the best part of two months, yet it was used to write that advert in the first place. An advert that was only placed last week. Who could have typed it except for you?'

Bertie spoke, but kept his eyes down at the floor, not wanting to look and meet Alice's. 'Did you realise, too late perhaps, that your typewriter was too incriminating?

Even with the lengths you went to in order to disguise your typing, by purposefully typing badly. The letters on your typewriter have worn uniquely to your machine – it's almost as distinctive as a fingerprint. Might you have switched machines in an attempt to draw attention away from your own?'

Bertie gave Alice a long interrogating stare. She returned his expression, not with one of fear or rage, but with one of deep curiosity.

'You are the one who invited me to be involved in this whole affair in the first place,' said Bertie. 'Could that have been your chance to influence the narrative, control the story? A way to force us to see things your way?'

Alice rolled her eyes. 'Well, yes, I'm sure that could have been the case *if* I'd been very clever about everything and planned this all out in advance. But Bertie, you've known me for years. Does planning something out meticulously in advance sound at all like something I could do?'

Bertie returned a warm smile as he thought about the chaos of Alice's desk. 'No. Thankfully it doesn't.'

'But that does bring us to something that we know to be true. Everything about this murder *was* planned out in advance,' interjected Hugh.

Bertie nodded. 'Hugh's right, it had to be. At the time, I thought you meant that it had been planned out in advance by a few days, maybe a week. But why shouldn't it have been planned out by twelve weeks or more, when the typewriter was still in the theatre? That meant the advert could have been typed ahead of time, conveniently letting suspicion fall on Alice if that piece of paper was ever found.'

'Finally, someone's seeing some sense,' Alice commented wryly, but with relief. She turned to face the others in the room. 'Any of you could have used my typewriter; you knew where it was. All of you.'

Hugh nodded in agreement. 'Which means the change of typewriter—'

Alice's eyes flashed with inspiration as she interrupted him. 'My typewriter was no longer at the theatre. That means whoever wrote that first note couldn't use it for the second.'

'Which means our murderer has to be someone who also had access, not only to your typewriter when it was at the theatre, but also to *this* typewriter,' said Hugh, indicating the incriminating machine on the table. Danny slid down into his seat, glumly.

'What was the purpose of the advert and then this second note?' Hugh asked the silent room. 'Was it a warning from our murderer? Or was it just from someone desperate to get the show called off?'

'You're talking about me, I suppose... I may as well admit it,' came Gareth James's voice. He cleared his throat. 'Yes. I stood to gain if the show hadn't have gone ahead, that much is true.'

Heads turned as the theatre manager spoke.

'It's why I wasn't exactly pushing for the show to go ahead on the day; I would have been happy to see it cancelled. It would have been to my benefit.'

'So *you* placed the advert?' asked Margo, impatiently, from behind him.

Gareth stood and turned to face Margo so he could answer. 'No. That wasn't me. I wasn't responsible for the follow-up note either. The situation could have been to my advantage but, even though I would have been pleased if the show was cancelled, I didn't push the matter. The show went ahead.'

'We're here to talk about murder,' said Hugh, gravely. 'Would that have been to your gain? Any performances would have almost certainly been cancelled after something like that. Saving you from losing everything...'

'Saving me from losing...' Gareth repeated, lost for words. 'I would have rather lost everything; I would have rather lost the theatre than become a killer. Just the thought of it...' He gave an involuntary shiver. 'I could never.' He was glad to retake his seat, if a little unsteadily, shaking his head.

'But there was another reason to send that note, aside from a warning or an attempt to get the show cancelled. It was Bertie's idea, really...' Hugh turned to Bertie, letting him continue the story.

'We thought... I thought...' Bertie corrected himself when Hugh gave him a sharp look. 'Where better for someone to disguise themselves than backstage at a theatre, where everyone is dressed up in over-the-top costumes and makeup already? More than that, the advert and subsequent note meant that there would be more people milling around the theatre than usual, more faces to be lost in.'

'Oh, that's very good,' commented Alice, impressed.

'It was all a distraction. It forced us to look for an outsider and made everyone drop their guard after the performance. Once we discovered that the advertised murder did not take place, everyone relaxed a little, making it the perfect time to strike.'

'Well, this is all very well,' called a voice from the back of the room. Margo stood there with her arms still folded. 'But who the hell did it then?'

Hugh put a hand up, encouraging her to fall silent. He nodded for Bertie to continue.

'I saw it for myself when I came into the auditorium on that first day. One person who was encouraging everyone to pull together, to make sure that the show *would* go ahead. The one person who, when you put the puzzle pieces in place, is the only person who could have had access to this second typewriter.'

Bertie swallowed before letting his eyes fall on the poised figure sat at the front of the group.

'Katherine Debenham.'

Chapter Twenty-Six

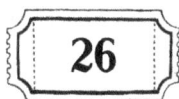

26

Katherine Debenham sat motionless and statuesque. Slowly the frozen expression began to thaw and the barest hint of a smile appeared at the corners of her mouth. She let her eyes fall effortlessly, first on Hugh, then on Bertie. She let her breath out sharply through her nose, an almost imperceptible snort of derision.

'Are you quite sure? Me? The one person who couldn't possibly have done it. Are you two feeling quite alright? I would never want to see harm come to my beloved Anthony.'

Bertie leaned back against the edge of a table, taking the weight off his feet. 'Ever since I arrived here, I've been told how loyal the Debenhams are to each other. What a strong couple they are, how they're still in love after all these years together. Margo was criticised widely, by an entire theatrical community, when she suggested there might be some kind of marital issues between the two of you. Those troubles were simply dismissed as a gambling habit, something which Anthony owned up to. Afterwards, because you had stood by him, it seemed like your marriage was stronger than ever before.'

At the back of the room, Bertie could see Margo shifting herself, trying to get a better view to see if there was any kind of reaction. Her efforts were in vain; Katherine Debenham hadn't moved a muscle during Bertie's speech.

'Despite this carefully crafted facade, I suspect your true relationship was much closer to the one presented in Alice's play – perhaps that's the reason you were able to act it so convincingly. Even your own servants admitted that you and your husband often led relatively separate lives in private.'

Katherine didn't turn to look at them, but behind her Elise and Arthur could both feel the bristle of her disapproval and shifted uncomfortably in their seats.

'Mr Carroll, we were both professionals in what can sometimes be a trying industry. Am I expected to sit here and listen to a lecture on an unconventional lifestyle – from you of all people?' Katherine Debenham's piercing look was wielded with the precision of a surgeon's scalpel, causing Bertie to fall silent.

Hugh took over the telling of the story. 'Recently, it seemed that Anthony Debenham's gambling was coming between the two of you, once again. There was the matter of the missing money – where had that gone, if not to cover his gambling debts? We know that Anthony had been meeting people away from the theatre, at his club. We know that there were evenings where he left the club in a bad mood. To onlookers, it might seem as if he was having a run of bad luck.'

Hugh began to wander aimlessly as he spoke, weaving between the tables. 'But what's interesting is *when* Mr Debenham's mood began to change. We thought it might have had something to do with the advert being placed, but the change had begun before then. Did his low mood begin when he was forced to take the money from his safe to cover his gambling losses, something which would surely be noticed by you? Or was there something else? There was another significant event that happened prior to the advert being placed, something very important. The conversation that was overheard by your driver. Arthur?' Hugh had arrived at the table of Arthur and Elise. He turned to address them. 'Could you tell us about the conversation you witnessed?'

Arthur started to speak, but the words didn't quite flow at first. He cleared his throat with a cough and began to speak with more clarity. 'Mrs Debenham accused Mr Debenham of stealing a large sum of money from the safe in the house.'

'And did Mr Debenham deny this?'

'Yes,' Arthur said, nodding. 'He said he had no idea what she was talking about.'

'Indeed, he didn't. In fact, despite what we thought we knew about him, he was never a big gambler.'

Arthur looked up at Hugh, confused. 'But the times he left the club, angry with himself?'

'This was the genius of Katherine Debenham's plan, but also it was the undoing. Throwing this accusation in front of you, she knew that it would get out. In the times before you drove for the Debenhams, you were always known for sharing some of the juicier gossip that you overheard with your other passengers.'

'I... Well, alright.' Arthur had started to defend himself, but quickly gave up. Everyone in the room already knew that it was true.

'It was an attempt to divert attention towards Anthony, the suggestion that he might be getting mixed up in something that could have led to trouble. After all, the gambling had worked so well as a distraction before.'

'Before?' said Arthur, not following the train of thought.

'Of course, he had always gambled from time to time, and people knew he did. It's why it had always made such a convincing cover story, but it was never to the extent that had been implied. A very clever idea, taking something real and then exaggerating it into a believable tale. It worked well last time. His small gambling habit was embellished, transforming it into something large enough that could have plausibly driven a wedge between a husband and a wife. All in order to hide the real truth of the matter.'

'And what was the truth of the matter?' asked John. The director sounded like he had something caught in his throat.

'That there really was an affair.'

John gave laugh of disbelief, although he wasn't quite as sure of himself as he had been previously. 'That's ridiculous, we know there was never an affair. Anthony would never...'

'He would, you know,' came Margo's voice, defiantly, from the back of the room. 'It was with me.' The admission caused a cacophony of chairs scraping as everyone turned around to look at her. The only exception was Katherine Debenham, who remained unresponsive at the front of the room.

'But it can't be...' John stuttered. 'I've been acquainted with the Debenhams for years. I would have known. There's no way I wouldn't have known.'

Hugh smiled, setting off from Arthur's table and pacing around the room again. 'Of course, Katherine and Anthony Debenham are two brilliant actors. The biggest role of their life was convincing everyone around them that they were a content and happy couple. I even believe that they had agreed to put the past behind them and move on from the matter. But nothing can last for ever, not even love. Not when it's built on a lie.'

'It wasn't a lie.' A quiet voice spoke near to Bertie. 'It wasn't a lie,' repeated Katherine again, this time with more power.

'No, I don't think it was,' said Bertie, sympathetically. 'I do believe you loved Anthony and were prepared to forgive him. You were prepared to stand by him, as long as something like that never happened again. But something *did* happen. There was another affair, but this time it wasn't on Anthony's side, it was yours.'

The look Katherine shot Bertie was so venomous it caused him to stand up, edging away from her. Now, from a safer distance, he continued.

'We knew there was someone else involved. There had to be.' Hugh had come to a stop by a table and rested an accusing hand on the shoulder of Danny Owen. 'The owner of our second typewriter.'

'The money. It wasn't Anthony who had taken it in order to gamble. It was you. You'd been spending it, keeping Danny Owen tucked away. Hugh and I came across a man who hasn't been able to hold a secure job for years, drinking expensive whisky, living in a brand-new apartment and smoking cigarettes from an expensive-looking case. Doesn't sound quite likely, does it?' said Bertie.

'Alright, Bertie,' said Danny, sounding defeated. 'You didn't have to go in on me like that.' He looked up at Hugh, still standing at his shoulder, who gave an apologetic kind of shrug.

'I don't know how long you've been … shall we say, romantically entangled? But we're pretty sure we know when you first met, isn't that right, Gertie?' Bertie looked across the room, catching the eye of his secretary, who had been watching closely.

'That's right. Duke of York's, 1932, *Call Me Back* by Alice Crawford,' she said, expertly recalling the information she had looked up.

Alice looked at Bertie, a little startled at the mention of her name.

'The play you couldn't remember anything about,' he prompted.

A look of enlightenment appeared on her face and she became enthusiastic as she started to recall the details. 'Yes, the one with the fingerprints. Sorry, finger-marks. Now I remember it, it was all about the impressions we leave behind, every touch leaves a trace. That was ever so clever of me.' Alice smiled smugly, but her face froze with sudden realisation, lifting a finger to point at Katherine. 'But of course, you were in it.' Her serious demeanour fell away as she turned to Gertie for more information. 'Did it get good reviews?'

The secretary nodded.

'Danny Owen was in the cast too,' Bertie said, delicately steering the conversation back to the point again. 'Your West End debut I believe?'

Danny smiled, remembering. 'Yes, not that I had terribly much to do. I sort of played this foppish character who swanned in and out of the room every now and then. Rather fun, I seem to remember. I got to wear all these stylish outfits.' His smile faded, not sure if he'd given something away.

'I expect you caught someone's eye,' Bertie said, casting a glance over to Katherine Debenham, who was watching him intently. 'I'm not sure if your affair started then, or perhaps later.'

Danny shook his head. 'You make it sound all so sordid, Bertie, but it wasn't like that. I've always found that people have taken to me, treated me kindly.'

'And what do you provide them in return?' Bertie asked, knowingly.

'I'm not sure I like what you're suggesting there,' Danny said, in a huff.

'I suspect that Mrs Debenham had a particular talent in influencing men to do what she wanted. There was Harry Shilling, for example. Someone who was already a shady character and the only person whose finger-marks appeared on the murder weapon.'

Bertie continued the explanation where Hugh left off. 'I'm sure you would have already known that Shilling was a fan of the theatre – a fan of yours. Had you seen him at the stage door before? Had you seen his drawings of you? You planned this murder months ago, using Alice's type-writer to type out the text of the advert to give to Shilling, manipulating him, convincing him to go and place it for you. He didn't really understand what it all meant; it didn't matter. What did you promise to reward him with, a chance to spend some time with you? It would be easy to invite him in as your guest. During the course of that meeting you might casually hand him the ornate letter opener while you tell him a story. After all, there was enough detail in Alice's play for you to understand the role that fingerprints play in an investigation and how you could avoid leaving your own behind.'

'But it was your careful handling of the knife that was

your undoing,' Hugh explained. 'It's not just the presence of finger-marks that is important; sometimes it's the absence of marks that tells a clearer story. No other finger-marks appeared on that letter opener, which was suspicious in itself. Something that would have been in daily use should have been covered in them. It was a clumsy attempt to try and frame someone else. And when you needed to send that second note, to try and force the theatre into taking things more seriously, Alice's typewriter wasn't available. You used Danny's typewriter to write the note and dropped it off to be discovered at the stage door. Now, while he might be a self-confessed pretty boy, I think he's also pretty smart. He had started to work out what was going on, at least part of it. Maybe in your haste, you hadn't been as discreet as you thought and he heard you typing. Maybe he even saw you.'

Danny remained still, slumped low in his chair, but this revelation caused Katherine to look startled. She managed to keep her emotions under control though, remaining still.

'I don't think you wanted to believe that the woman you were having an affair with could be a murderer. In fact, you still might not believe it.'

'I *can't* believe it, Bertie, I just can't...' Danny said, his voice laced with emotion.

'But she did. She pre-emptively accused Anthony of taking the money to gamble with before he had a chance to discover it was missing for himself. He knew it didn't make any sense. He knew for a fact he hadn't taken it.

From the moment the plan was set in action and the cover-up, to disguise the fact his wife had been keeping someone on the side, was revealed in front of their driver, Anthony's fate was sealed. Those people that he was visiting at the club, they weren't men chasing down gambling debts; they were friends or people he trusted, reporting back on his wife's movements. He was trying to solve the mystery himself, but he didn't manage to do it before he was murdered.'

Bertie shook his head. 'We were mistaken for a long time. There was a visitor at the theatre who we thought was there to see Anthony. When we saw Dennis deliver the message that there was a visitor, he had come to Anthony's dressing room. Not because that's where Mr Debenham would be, but because he knew that's where his wife would be. Dennis has always told us that he always knows where everyone is. The message was really for Katherine, but because it was Anthony we heard interrupting the message and telling them to be sent away, we incorrectly assumed that the visitor was for him. It wasn't.'

Hugh looked at Danny, who appeared to be sobbing quietly. 'It was you, wasn't it, Mr Owen? You had come to try and see Mrs Debenham. You suspected that she might have had something planned. You realised that the newspaper advert was no joke and you were afraid that she would try something. You wanted to stop her, and you may have very nearly succeeded in doing so. That's why you came to Romano's later too, to keep a close eye on her.'

Danny nodded jerkily, the tears now freely falling. 'I'm a nobody. I couldn't... I knew I had a good thing going with Katherine, but the idea that someone would kill for me...'

'And is that what you did, Mrs Debenham? Kill, so you could be with your young lover?'

A wry smile appeared across Katherine's face. 'That's all very good, both of you, but this is a fantasy of a playwright and his detective friend. Everyone knows there's no way I could have possibly killed him.'

'Ah yes, well, Bertie managed to think of the solution mere moments before me, so I'll let him do the explaining,' Hugh said, with a proud voice.

Bertie looked a little sheepish before he began. 'It was actually Gertie who put me on to it. She did it with a book, but perhaps we'll use this booth to demonstrate instead.'

He walked over to where Gertie and Dennis were sitting, signalling to one of the waiters, who deposited a tray with an open bottle of champagne and two glasses.

Bertie picked up one of the glasses and the bottle. 'After the show I walked past Anthony on my way up to Gareth's office. He seemed in good spirits.' Bertie held up the bottle, making his point. 'A celebration was in order. He called down to you, Katherine, saying that he'd be down in a moment. Was that your idea, or his?'

Bertie looked directly at Katherine, waiting for an answer, but none came.

'We'll assume it was yours,' he said and began pouring the first glass of champagne. When it was half full, he placed it on the table in front of Gertie. 'Why not? When everything had gone so well, as you knew it would.'

He had finished pouring the second glass and went to put it down in front of Dennis, whose eyes were wide with anticipation. Bertie hesitated, pulling the glass back and giving Dennis a look to let him know that he shouldn't drink it. He set the glass down delicately in front of the young man, who looked at it a little glumly.

'We know the murder was planned, because there was no struggle, there was no noise. Too tidy, I think you said, Hugh. But how easy would it have been for you to slip a large dose of Veranol into your husband's drink, something which we knew you used from time to time. Not enough to kill him, but in the next fifteen to twenty minutes it would be enough to make him drowsy, make it easy for you to overpower him and to use the letter opener to lethal effect. I don't know if Anthony was already dead by the time you left the room to meet Margo, but he would be soon.'

Margo spoke up, quietly, her voice shaking a little. 'But the room was empty, Bertie. There was no one there.'

'Quite a neat trick, wasn't it? Inviting someone to dinner, who was known to dislike you publicly, to provide your alibi. There was no reason for her to cover for you, no reason for her to lie. I'm sorry, Margo, you were mistaken. Katherine's dressing room was not empty when you came back to the theatre. Just like this booth, not only did it contain two empty champagne glasses, but also a dead body with a dagger in his neck.'

'It was, I promise you—'

Bertie held up a hand to silence her. 'It was Gertie who solved it really, with her pile of books all stacked up on top of each other. You returned to the theatre to collect Katherine Debenham's coat. But instead of collecting it from here,' Bertie said, pointing to the booth where the champagne glasses were still sitting and waiting, 'why not collect your coat from over there?'

Bertie turned to the identical booth along from Gertie and Dennis. There was nothing in it, except Hugh's coat, which had been lying innocently across the table since they had arrived. A ripple of understanding rolled across some of the others in the restaurant.

'They were always in and out of each other's dressing rooms, the loving couple,' said Bertie, with a note of bitterness in his voice. 'One person's belongings were often found in the others. That's what you said, isn't it, Dennis?' Bertie looked at the call boy for confirmation and he duly nodded in return.

'Like identical books stacked up on top of each other, every floor of the theatre is also identical, with identically sized dressing rooms. That's why Katherine had to insist on not taking the star dressing room and instead take a room that would match her husband's. On the last day of a show, as things begin to be packed up ready to be removed, there are fewer personal items out on display. Perhaps, with the lights off, it would have been almost impossible to tell that it wasn't Katherine's dressing room that you visited. It was Anthony's.'

Margo stood looking curiously at Bertie. 'But I could have sworn...' she said, not quite ready to believe the story.

'Why else take the lift to go up one floor?' Bertie asked her. 'Why not take the stairs? It was to disguise the fact that, in reality, you were going up two floors. Katherine talked at you the entire time, distracting you in an attempt to make sure you didn't notice. And you didn't. There are no numbers on the dressing rooms and Anthony Debenham's name tag could be easily removed, leaving no giveaway signs of whose room it really was. You took it for granted you were looking into Katherine Debenham's dressing room – after all, you saw her retrieve her own coat from inside it – while all the time, Anthony was already lying dead one floor below.'

'Is that true, Mrs Debenham?' Hugh asked coldly.

A hush fell across the room, while they waited for Katherine to respond.

'Oh yes.' She spoke in a calm voice as she rose slowly from her seat. With everyone else remaining still and silent, her quiet words filled the room. 'The playwright and the detective,' she said, looking at each of them with a piercing stare, 'and their collection of silly little friends...'

She cast her eye around the room, deliberately letting her eyes linger for a moment on Alice, then Gertie.

'I thought I was being so clever, too.' She spoke in an

intense, measured way, as if she was trying to stop herself from exploding. Eventually she failed. 'Damn you!' she cried, making everyone jump. 'Damn every last one of you!'

Chapter Twenty-Seven

27

In response to Katherine Debenham's outburst, Hugh quickly raised his hand, directing the constables waiting nearby to move in, but Bertie put his hand out to stop him.

'I'm interested, though. When did the idea of murder occur to you? Before you started work on this play? Is that why you asked your agent to insist that you both booked this job?' He asked the question delicately, taking a few steps towards the actress. She struggled to contain a smile. She was proud, in a way, of her work and to be asked questions about it, like she was being quizzed by an interviewer for a magazine article about a role she had played. As she spoke, the smile returned occasionally, flashing awkwardly across her lips.

'No. That was just one of those little things that fell

into place quite neatly. It was your play really, Alice.' She turned to address the playwright directly. 'Such a disappointing ending, in a way. In it, I make all the plans for the perfect murder, but then never go through with it. Rather unsatisfactory, if you ask me. Well, when I saw your typewriter unattended one day, I thought *why not write my own story*? And so I did. I think it was a rather good one too, although I should really ask the opinion of a critic or a playwright, shouldn't I?'

She turned to Bertie, waiting for him to offer his opinion, but he refused.

'Involving Margo—' he started, but was interrupted by Katherine.

'No, you're right. I should have killed her too, the little bitch. Killing really is easy once you get used to the idea of it. I used her to provide the perfect alibi. I really thought that would do the trick, having it come from an enemy. Still, it was thrilling to look into the eyes of the silly little girl who tried to tear our marriage apart, knowing that all the time her lover was already dead.'

Katherine took a step forward, then another, although not in the direction of Margo, on whom she kept her back turned. She spoke over her shoulder.

'Did you think it was love?' she spat, mocking in a childlike voice. 'Did you think that you were special? Of course, I understand now. When you do find love, you'll do anything you can to protect it.' She stopped behind Danny, resting a tender hand on his shoulder. He didn't seem to register the touch, remaining silent with his face hidden in his hands. 'Isn't that right, darling?' she added in a haunting voice as she let her fingers caress the back of his neck. Danny slowly dropped his hands to the table, revealing a tear-streaked face.

'This?' he finally managed to choke out in disbelief. 'For love? Is that what you... I just thought I was onto a good thing. A few trinkets, some nice clothes, all in return for...' He didn't finish the sentence, shaking his head as he struggled to get everything straight. It was very nearly comical. 'You think that's love?' he said, with an incredulous laugh.

Katherine whipped her hand from his shoulder, as if she had been burned. She looked around the room skittishly, sensing everyone's eyes on her. As an actress, the feeling of an audience's eyes on her had always brought a sense of warmth and comfort; now their sharp stares had the opposite effect, leaving her with a decided chill. She gave an involuntary shiver as two constables approached on Hugh's command.

It took every ounce of her remaining strength to regain her composure. The usual poise and air of elegance she had always carried during her long career reappeared on the surface; so sudden was the change in expression, it was quite unnerving. However, there was something different about her; Bertie could see the fire and passion that drives a brilliant performer had somehow faded.

The constable closest to her reached out his arm towards her shoulder, so that he could escort her from the room. She shrugged it off, remaining rooted to the spot, refusing to let herself be manhandled in such a manner. The constable gave her a kind, almost pleading look, and she relented – allowing herself to be guided from the room with a gentle hand on the back of her arm.

As she disappeared through the front doors and out of sight, there would be no final words, no curtain call. There was just an uneasy silence. The room sat frozen for nearly a minute, no one daring to breathe out. It was John Tay who broke the stillness first, moving over to Danny's table and kneeling next to him, providing some mumbled words of comfort that no one else was able to hear.

Hugh gave Bertie's shoulder a squeeze in thanks, before he followed the two policemen out onto the street.

Dennis gave a beaming smile to Bertie as he approached his booth. Gertie's smile was almost as wide. 'Well, that was very impressive, Mr Carroll,' she said, sliding the still-full glass of champagne across the table to him.

'I'm not sure celebrations are in order; I feel a little wrung out by all of this.' Bertie paused a moment, eyeing the glass. 'Oh hell, I could use the drink,' he said, lifting the glass and taking a generous gulp.

Alice approached the table, looking serious. 'Do you really think that Katherine thought the end of my play was a let-down?'

'I'm not sure we should be trusting Katherine Debenham's judgement on anything.' Bertie let out a sigh of relief. He smiled at Alice. 'I thought the end of your play was wonderful.'

'Well, thank goodness for that,' she said, picking up the glass in front of Dennis and downing it in one. 'I think we need some more of this before the night is out. Here's to another murder mystery solved by the brilliant Bertie Carroll,' she said, raising her now empty glass in a toast.

'I couldn't have done it without your help, Alice. Gertie as well, and of course, you too, Dennis.' He addressed each one of them in turn with a thankful smile. 'Hugh did pretty well too,' he added, looking thoughtfully towards the entrance through which his friend had just exited.

'I don't suppose you would be willing to provide a comment?' Margo's voice came from behind the group, causing them all to turn. She held an open notebook up in explanation. 'For the paper?'

'Oh, for goodness' sake, Margo. Can't you take a night off for once in your life?' said Alice, sounding exasperated.

Margo shrugged. 'Honestly, I don't really know what else to do.'

Alice raised an eyebrow. 'Why not come for a drink with us? Take your mind off it.'

'You know what,' said Margo, closing her notebook. 'I might just do that.'

Bertie emerged onto the street just in time to see a police car depart. Hugh was about to climb into a second to follow closely behind but stopped when he saw Bertie standing there.

'Harry Shilling, Hugh. What about him?'

Hugh spoke seriously. 'I don't know, Bertie. We've not heard anything about him for a while now.'

'"Killing really is easy once you get used to the idea of it." That's what she said. Could she have killed multiple people? Might he be another victim? If it was Katherine who tried to kill me on the Underground, might she try to do away with her unwitting accomplice as well, to cover her tracks?'

'It's a strong possibility.'

'I don't want him to become forgotten in all this.'

'I promise you, we'll find out what happened to him.'

'You can't promise that,' said Bertie, sadly. 'The truth is, we may never know. We may never find him.'

'What I can promise you is that I'll do everything I can.'

Bertie smiled. 'Yes, you can promise me that.'

Exiting from the restaurant, Alice saw Bertie and called over. 'We'll see you there?'

Bertie gave a gentle nod.

'See you where?' Hugh asked, looking past him at the others who were spilling out of Romano's onto the street.

'We're all going over to Betty's. A bit of a celebratory drink, you know.'

'Right.' Hugh breathed out disapprovingly, although he only seemed half serious.

'You'd be welcome to come too, Hugh. It's just going to be drinks and talking, nothing untoward, nothing outrageous.'

Hugh looked towards the waiting police car. 'I'm going to be tied up with this for some time.'

'After then?'

'Perhaps,' he relented.

Bertie returned a half-smile, but all the time knowing that he would never come. 'Well, I'll see you there or... Wherever. Maybe at your next fight – the boxing?'

Hugh smiled, giving a small chuckle. 'You know what? I was thinking I might give something else a go. Football, perhaps. The force has an excellent team.'

'And I'm sure you'd be brilliant at it too.' Bertie paused. 'Please stay in touch, won't you?'

'Of course I will,' said Hugh, truthfully. Bertie knew that he meant it.

With a nod of farewell, Hugh hopped into the waiting police car, and it shot off into the distance.

Bertie turned, finding the collection of actors, writers, crew and assorted theatre people watching on and waiting for him to join them. Some of the crew at the theatre had heard what was going on down the road and had walked over from the theatre to see if they could find out the news, including Sam, who was waiting, leaning casually against a nearby lamppost. He gave a broad smile and joined the rest of the group as they set off in the direction of Betty's.

Alice hung back, waiting for Bertie. 'Come on, let's go, shall we?'

He walked into her open arms for a congratulatory hug, finding comfort in the warm embrace. They linked arms and joined behind the others, remaining a few steps behind.

'I'm terribly worried, Bertie. When Katherine said she got the idea from my play...'

'You're worried that you've inspired a murderer?'

'Yes, and I feel bloody awful about it.'

'The one thing I've learned in all these years is that you can only take responsibility for yourself; you can't take responsibility for the actions of anyone else.' He stopped and turned to look back at the road where Hugh had just driven away.

Alice stopped, speaking seriously. 'You remember what we said, the other day? We don't get the privilege of writing our own stories. This is real life, not a play. We can't always write the endings that we want.'

Bertie sighed. 'While I think that is probably true, I don't want to believe it. Not really.'

'So, what shall we do about our ending today?' said Alice, turning and guiding Bertie to join her as they trailed behind the group of people who were slowly making their way down the Strand.

The all too familiar outline of the Gaiety rose up in front of them.

'I think we should have an uplifting one, don't you?'

The Gaiety Theatre
(and other theatrical locations in this book)

As with all fiction, a little bit of artistic licence has had to take place to help the plot run smoothly.

This book is set at the Gaiety Theatre, which was located at the end of the Strand in London. This Gaiety was actually the second Gaiety Theatre, the first being across the road on the site of the Strand Musick Hall.

In 1902 a whole swathe of London was swept away to create Aldwych, named after the old Wych Street, and several theatres would be lost as part of this development. In addition to the first Gaiety, the Olympic, the Globe and the Opera Comique would all be demolished. However, three new theatres would eventually be built replace them: the Waldorf (now the Novello), the Aldwych and the new Gaiety – which opened four months after the original theatre closed in 1903.

The Gaiety Restaurant was built at the same time as the theatre and still stands today as Marconi House, where the first BBC radio service was broadcast from. Because of their closeness, the Gaiety Theatre became notable as being the first theatre to have a performance be broadcast live from it. It is rumoured that someone had the bright idea when they could hear a production in progress through the wall that the two buildings shared!

The theatre opened with a production of *The Orchid*. However, the night before the new theatre opened there was a shout of 'Fire!' and the show's playwright, James Tanner, leaped into action pulling the lever to activate "the drencher". This system is designed to pour water down the back of the safety curtain, keeping it cool and ensuring that it can do its job – keeping a fire contained backstage while the audience can be safely evacuated.

The controls for the drencher are usually located next to the safety curtain, which – in the UK anyway – must be raised and lowered during every performance. Despite clear labelling – and usually much additional signage added over the years as a warning to the operator – the drencher will still sometimes get released accidentally instead of the safety curtain, releasing countless gallons of water onto the stage.

Then as it would now, once James Tanner had pulled the lever, chaos promptly ensued. Scenery and performers were soaked, and the orchestra pit began to fill up with water – which contained a full complement of very unimpressed musicians who had unfortunately been rehearsing at the time. Despite this minor setback, the show still opened to huge success the following night, attended by King Edward VII and Queen Alexandra.

In 1939 it was announced that the theatre, along with the nearby Lyceum, would be demolished to make way for a new road layout. The final performance at the Gaiety was on the 25th February that year. Thankfully demolition of both theatres was avoided when the road widening scheme was abandoned.

However, only a few months later it was announced that the Gaiety was going to be replaced by an office building and much of the interior was stripped. The Second World War interrupted these plans and once again the demolition of the theatre was avoided. By now it was in a pretty derelict condition, only made worse by the bomb damage it received during the Blitz.

Performer Lupino Lane bought the shell of the building in 1946 with the intention of bring it back to life. However, the damage over the years was more significant than first thought and repair costs began spiralling out of control. In 1957, nearly twenty years since the theatre had seen its last performance and after surviving two previous demolition attempts, the Gaiety's history finally came to an end when it was sold on to be replaced by an office building. Today a luxury hotel sits on the site.

Romano's, The Era Buildings and Harker's Paint Studio are all real locations which, at one time, were all connected to the theatrical world.

Like the Gaiety, Romano's was bomb damaged during the Blitz and the building was eventually replaced by today's Stanley Gibbons building, located next to the Vaudeville Theatre.

The Era Buildings still retain a theatrical connection as the offices of Charles Fox, long-standing suppliers of makeup to the theatre and TV industries.

Harker's Paint Studio remained in continuous use for its original purpose until 2018. Flints – a supplier of theatrical paints and ironmongery – operated out of the building for thirty years, but eventually outgrew the premises and moved to a larger warehouse in Deptford.

Despite its Grade II listed status and fierce campaigning from the theatrical community, the building was sold to be redeveloped into flats. A tragedy, not only because of the historical interest of this unique place, but also because the paint frame was still in regular use by scenic artists (the number of purpose-built facilities for painting large backdrops and cloths for theatre are now vanishingly small).

I couldn't resist putting in a lost London Underground location as well – Aldwych Station. This station also has a theatre connection, being built on the site of one. There had been a theatre located here since 1832, but was rebuilt in 1882 due to safety concerns. This new Royal Strand Theatre ran successfully for twenty years until it was bought by the Great Northern, Piccadilly and Brompton Railway to build the station. It closed in 1994.

Danny Owen's flat is inspired by the Isokon Building

in Belsize Park. Agatha Christie and her husband Max Mallowan moved into this building at the height of the Blitz, when their own house had been damaged by bombing. Christie was a prolific writer during the war, writing several novels and short stories from this address. In keeping with our other theatrical connections, this was also the period where Christie adapted several works for the stage. *And Then There Were None*, *Appointment with Death* and *Murder on the Nile* were all plays that were written here. It was also where she wrote an original play for radio called *Three Blind Mice*, which would go on to become the basis for *The Mousetrap* – still the world's longest running play.

While the Gaiety is one of London's many "lost" theatres, there is some good news – it hasn't been completely lost. Some original interior features of the theatre were saved and installed in The Victoria pub, Paddington. A perfect place to raise a glass to the memory of these wonderful buildings and the theatre people who worked in them.

Acknowledgements

This book is dedicated to the Gaiety boys and girls who entertained thousands over the years at the first Gaiety Theatre on the Strand, and when they moved a short distance to the other side of the road to the second Gaiety Theatre, where this book is set.

My dedication to love, laughter and happy ever after is a nod to Lupino Lane, who did his best to save the Gaiety. He was the producer and star of *Me and My Girl*, which opened at the Victoria Palace Theatre in 1937 and was a huge success. It ran for over 1,600 performances and was revived several times in the following years. It seems fitting that many pages of this book were written or edited on the fly floor at the Victoria Palace during my quiet breaks at work and posters for this musical are still proudly displayed around the theatre.

Me and My Girl made Lupino Lane a small fortune, much of which he would use to purchase the shell of the Gaiety after it had been bombed in the Second World War, in an attempt to revive it and save the theatre. Sadly, he was unsuccessful and the theatre was demolished.

The work of protecting theatres still continues today by the Theatres Trust, whose archives and library are always useful when researching the lost theatres I use in this series of books.

Thank you to my husband, Stuart, whose expertise in working out whodunnit is invaluable when he gets to read an early draft of the book for the first time. Huckleberry, our miniature dachshund, is not as good at solving murders but his quiet comfort, as he snoozes nearby while I type out each page, is treasured.

A huge thank you goes out to Mary Torjussen, who edited this book with such care and enthusiasm. Her contributions and comments have undoubtably made this story better in every way. Thanks also to Nicola Bigwood for her proofreading services and making sure that this book arrives into your hands in the very best shape.

Victoria Hyde at Insta Book Tours, and all the bloggers who have embraced my books, continue to be a wonderful support. Special thanks goes to my book tour bloggers: Alice, Amy, Andrew, Ben, Cathy, Chloe, Deborah, Diane, Emma D, Emma N, Fiona, Georgina, Jasmin, Jess, Kath, Kerry, Laura D, Laura D, Mia, Neha, Samantha, Sarah, Stephanie H, Stephanie O, Tayla, Vickie, Victoria and Wendy.

Thank you to my fellow authors William Hussey, J.M. Hall, Orlando Murrin, Fiona Leitch, Greg Mosse, Kitty Murphy, A.J. West, Ian Moore and Tom Mead who have been generous enough to support this book with their kind words. I hope you will return their generosity on my behalf by buying their books!

She might not represent me, but thank you to literary agent Maddalena Cavaciuti at DHA. The conversation we had together whizzed past far too quickly, but her razor-sharp insight and feedback guided this book in a new direction.

Gemma Curtis has produced a wonderful linocut for the cover of this book. She is a brilliant artist and all her prints are available by searching for *WildWaterArtStore* online. The original prints for both this book and *Death on the Pier* hang on my wall with pride.

Finally, thanks to my readers, including those who have been kind enough to leave reviews, engage with me online and even sign up to my mailing list – so I can tell you when the next book is coming out! That someone takes the time to read my words, bringing to life these characters and settings in their own unique way, will always be a thrill to me.

Bertie and Hugh will return...

*Be the first to hear when by signing up
to the mailing list at
jamiewest.co.uk*